# House of
# DE ZAVALA
## The Legacy of the Black Heart Stone

*Praise for House of De Zavala*

"Texas is known for its tall tales and amazing true stories. Mike Lowrie skillfully weaves both into a captivating yarn about treasure hunting and the devastating cost of greed. His story is about Luis De Zavala, a proud descendant of Lorenzo De Zavala and founding father of Texas.

Like his ancestor, Luis is not one to back down from a good fight and for standing up for what he feels is right. His ethics are put to the test when he encounters a story told by his grandfather, Sergio De Zavala.

The story of an artifact of lost Aztec gold and the death, in a plane crash, of the Texas dentist who discovered the gold leads Luis into becoming an archaeologist, determined to dig up not only the past, but the truth.

Mike Lowrie takes the reader on a journey across Texas and into the borderlands of Mexico as Luis—along with his brother and beautiful fiancée, Amelia—try to stay one step ahead of the authorities in their quest to unravel the mysteries of a legendary treasure, and the curses that follow those who desire it."

—*Rebecca Huffstutler Norton*
*Executive Director, Frontier Times Museum, Bandera, Texas*

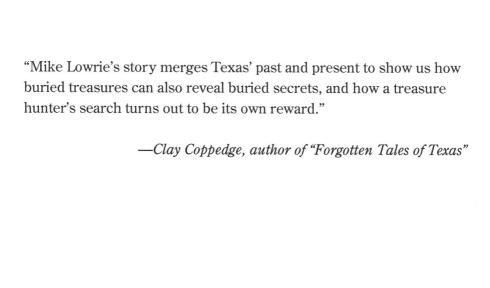

"Mike Lowrie's story merges Texas' past and present to show us how buried treasures can also reveal buried secrets, and how a treasure hunter's search turns out to be its own reward."

—*Clay Coppedge, author of "Forgotten Tales of Texas"*

Also by Mike Lowrie:
*Texas Tall Short Stories,* Elm Grove Publishing, 2021

# House of
# DE ZAVALA
## The Legacy of the Black Heart Stone

## Mike Lowrie

ISBN: 978-1-958407-09-7 (Hardback)

ISBN: 978-1-958407-10-3 (Soft Cover)

*Cover photo by Wade Lowrie and Mick Prodger
featuring Mark Garza*

*Portrait of Lorenzo de Zavala "Una Sociedad de Amigos",
Public domain via Wikimedia Commons*

Book design by designpanache

## ELM GROVE PUBLISHING

San Antonio, Texas, USA
www.elmgrovepublishing.com

Elm Grove Publishing is a legally registered trade name of Panache Communication Arts, Inc.

# Contents

# Preface

This story is about Luis De Zavala, a young archaeologist, and his quest for the preservation of historic artifacts. Artifacts that are sometimes referred to as buried treasure.

The House of De Zavala is not about a single treasure per se, but a collection of five treasures, each with their own adventures. They are in fact, five stories based on true events.

Wise men will tell you that the actual treasures are never worth as much as the bonds we build between our friends and family. The relationship between Luis and his grandfather was more of an apprenticeship than anything else. These were the lessons taught to Luis and his younger brother Tony.

This story is about the third generation of descendants of Lorenzo De Zavala—a rising political figure in his time. He was a statesman of the Republic of Texas and died in 1836. One thing is clear, Louis De Zavala did not descend from the average family with the usual misfortunes and accomplishments. Far from being average, the De Zavalas were caught up in one exciting adventure after another.

Luis De Zavala began his adult life as a college graduate fresh out of the University of Texas at San Antonio with a degree in archeology. Over time he developed an obsession around his work—to be an adamant crusader for the cause of preserving antiquities. His second obsession became his personal nemesis by the name of Dr. Andrew Wilson, also an archaeologist from the State of Texas Archaeological Division.

No acts of honor, heroism, or virtues of men were assumed or gifted to the De Zavalas. Luis and Tony earned their way to command by their own personal trials and tribulations.

The lesson that their grandfather laid before them, first as child-hood suggestions and then again as they grew older, became clear and concise words of advice. In the beginning of the book and until the end, it was always emphasized, "Beware the greed of men who sell their souls for the shine of gold. And beware of spirits that watch over those treasures you may seek."

Ironic that Luis became an archaeologist, seeking, digging, and acquiring those very things that his life-long teachings were meant for. Call it coincidence or a clear and concise plan of action, that's where Luis De Zavala landed—prepared for the treasure hunt.

Texas doesn't have any gold or silver mines of any significance, not like the western states that have the bragging history of strikes like the Comstock Lode in Nevada or the forty-niner strike in California.

This inevitably brings the curious to question a common proc-lamation that treasure hunters have been telling each other for years, "Texas has more buried treasure than any other state."

Some legends generate their own treasure stories—rumors re-ally. Stories of buried treasures never to have been unearthed because, quite frankly, there was never such treasure in the first place. They be-gan as wild unfounded tales—stories usually originating from the town drunk, probably in some bar.

It's a good thing to know if you're a tourist somewhere. If a local tries to sell you a map that says "X marks the spot," then you'd better treat it with a healthy amount of skepticism. There's a good chance it's a snipe hunt.

In reality, archaeologists spend the majority of their time not digging in the ground, but in academic research. The libraries, church archives, and museums are their main sources of information. That is our modern day archaeologist.

Let it never be forgotten, there are still wild prospectors out there in the world who still seek that pot of gold and will do anything to get it. As men become older and bolder, they sometimes give in to the sin of greed, often destroying everything they know that was good.

Sergio often reminded Luis and his brother Tony of the foundation from which they were born, that of their great-great-grandfather, Lorenzo De Zavala. In a way, Sergio had always considered the De Zavalas to be from a noble lineage.

This story is considered historical fiction, but Lorenzo De Zavala did actually exist. And so was—or is—the existence of the five stories about treasure that are incorporated in this book. Four of the stories are documented. You can find them in treasure hunting books.

The fifth story, about the Golden Aztec Eagle Warrior, is not documented anywhere. The one who knows the most about the statue is me, and I've never seen it. Nor have I even gotten close enough to see it. Every person involved with it is now dead. All of them.

The treasure map disappeared years ago, and quite frankly, that has led me to question whether it ever existed in the first place. But I do know this: the story I was told was compelling beyond belief. I asked a certain prospector to tell me the story again and again. I was told the story about the Golden Aztec Eagle Warrior four times in intricate detail and it never did waiver.

Over a period of many years I knew the story would be worth retelling someday, so I filed it away in my memory and later incorporated it into this book. Did the cave with the Eagle Warriors really exist? I don't know, but then again, I'm not a treasure hunter. I'm a story teller. And this is a good story to tell.

The stories about buried treasures in this book are considered to be unobtainable for one reason or another. So if you fancy grabbing a shovel from your garage and entertain the thought of digging random holes somewhere, I urge you to get some psychological counseling first or you'll drive yourself crazy digging holes.

It's impossible to tell anyone about the De Zavala story without emphasizing that it doesn't take place in any traditional or exotic location. Not in Hollywood, on top of the Eiffel Tower, or the pyramids in Egypt. It takes place right here in the Lone Star State with the historic city of San Antonio as the centerpiece. That is our exotic location.

It's also impossible to ignore the cultural traditions we have here in this part of Texas when reading this book. We congregate around our campfires and tell each other unfathomable stories. Texas believes in its independence. Some of us still practice chivalry and protest the absence of such virtues. The same can be said for the concept of honor and patriotism. We are a proud people that know we don't have the highest mountains or the most alligators, but we do know we've got a little of everything and the most of many precious things.

Each and every person in the state of Texas is what makes us who we are – boastful and proud.

*ML*

# 1.

## Reagan Canyon Part I — 2015
## Brewster County, West Texas

One of the few skills I left high school with was the ability to run. I was on the track team at South San High School and ran cross country. All I had to do was get lined out in a straight direction, and once I found my pace, I could run like the wind.

When you run for pleasure, endorphins are released into the brain and nervous system, causing what many would describe as a feeling of well-being, and that's the effect running had on me. Of course, running from the drug cartel in a remote place like Reagan Canyon was a totally different situation. I was running for my life, and that was not fun.

My supervisor warned me not to cross the Rio Grande to the Mexican side, but the lure of that little one-room *cantina* was just too tempting. It was the only man-made structure I had seen in two days of hunting for archaeological sites in the Trans-Pecos region, and the temptation overcame me.

The more parched my mouth became, the more I looked for an excuse to cross the river.

"Surely, they have something cold to drink over there," I thought to myself. "Just one little beer couldn't possibly cause any harm, right?"

It sounded simple, but as most people know, sometimes things aren't exactly what they appear to be.

Once I crossed, all I had a chance to do was order one beer and ask one question. I even asked it in Spanish to make them feel I was one of them, but they wouldn't have any of it. That's all it took for those Mexicans to pull out their guns and point them at me.

I didn't ask to see their membership cards, but I was reasonably sure that they were card-carrying cartel members. In fact, after they told me they wanted to cut my head off and display it at a local roadside park for all to see, it didn't take a genius to see that they were a bunch of mean bastards. To this day, I still don't know exactly why they suddenly got so pissed at me. I was in the middle of a hive of killer bees and before I could take the first sip of my beer, I was doing my best to get the hell out of there as fast as I could.

It all went south when the bartender and his two friends drew their pistols and pointed them at me. Without thinking and totally out of character, I hit the bartender over the head with my full beer and busted it all over his face. During the shock of the hit, I grabbed the hammer of the cocked pistol from the second man, spun him around, and put him in an instant choke hold. That caused the third man to accidentally pop off a round in my direction, hitting the man I was choking in the stomach.

It all happened in the blink of an eye. All three Mexicans stood there, frozen in place: the bartender with beer and glass in his face, the first bandit with a bullet hole in his stomach, and the third bandit frozen in disbelief that he had shot his *compadre*.

That was just enough chaos for me to dart out the front door, but that was only the beginning of my troubles. When I got outside and looked around, my ATV was gone. It was stolen by one of the locals. It was time to start running.

The situation forced me to head for the river as fast as I could. When I reached the banks of Texas soil, where I thought it'd be safe, I heard gunshots behind me and then bullets zipped over the top of my head. That scared the holy crap out of me, so I kept running.

The chase didn't end when the Mexicans reached the Rio Grande either. Those assholes crossed right behind me in a jeep and began to close the gap. I was out-manned and outclassed by everyone behind me. Most importantly, I never got that drink of water that I desperately needed. My water bottles and canteen were on my ATV that was stolen. I was a man running for his life through the desert with no assets.

As soon as I crested the banks of the Rio Grande and got up high enough, I looked at miles and miles of desert to the north and pessimistically evaluated my options.

With no trees big enough to make shade, the cactus and creosote bushes didn't offer any cover since they only grew knee-high. There was no place to hide on a landscape of flat desert ground.

By that time, I considered the situation to be a no-brainer—those guys were going to kill me if they caught me. The way I saw it, I had only one option. I had to make it to that first gully of Reagan Canyon before they did. If I could beat them to the first gully, they wouldn't be able to follow me in their jeep.

I was going to give it everything I could, but in the back of my mind I knew there was a good chance I would succumb to the heat. Plain and simple.

That first gully of Reagan Canyon was one deep and treacherous washout in the middle of the desert floor. There was no choice but to plunge myself down one of the walls of the washout, sliding down the steep rock wall on my butt until I reached the bottom. When I hit the bottom, I followed the windy washed-out path downstream, looking for a place to climb out.

The cartel Mexicans were forced to ditch their jeep as I predicted they would, but since I was apparently a priority to kill, they sent three men on foot to chase me through that winding washout.

After spending about fifteen minutes walking down the gravel bed, I was under the impression that they might be giving up, but I heard footsteps in the gravel bed behind me echo down the walls of the gully.

That's when I decided I had the advantage. If I could get out of the gully and make it to the top of the desert floor, I could probably outrun them on the flat ground. The only problem was I didn't know how much farther I could go with no water, and the heat was starting to take its toll.

I was already exhausted when I made the climb up out of the gully. Every step was a conscious effort that took more strength from me. When I reached the top, I faced to the north, lined out my stride, and found a good pace.

At about four hundred yards from the edge of the gully, more bullets zipped by my head and some hit the ground next to me. I had no other choice but to put some distance between me and them, so I quickened my pace and increased my stride.

After the first mile I realized that I was all alone. No one knew where I was, and my ability to make sound decisions was fading. I couldn't seem to remember my strategy anymore. I had escaped the immediate threat of the Mexican drug cartel, but now I had to deal with the conditions I found myself in. It was the harsh elements of the desert that were, quite frankly, kicking my ass.

At some point I completely forgot that the cartel was after me because all I could think of was how terribly hot it was.

It seemed like an eternity, but I made it an additional half mile. That's when my body hit the wall—a term runners use when they can't take another step. It was like someone pulled the drain plug on my energy reserves, followed by a wave of extreme nausea. My legs became uncontrollably shaky, causing me to collapse to my knees and fall over on my side. I stopped sweating. There was no shade.

Helplessly, I lay there and let the sun bake me. Then the thoughts of my own mortality crept into my mind.

"It won't be long now," I thought to myself. "I'm totally played out."

My nose and cheek were in the dirt. Aware of my surroundings, but panting, trying to catch my breath. I became unable to blink. My eyes became glazed over and my throat was so parched I was unable to swallow.

The elements were having their way with me as my mind drifted to when I was a kid swimming in the cool waters of the Medina River.

Fading into this unfamiliar realm, I feared that I might go insane before I made the final journey.

It was so unbearably hot.

That's what it's like when you're at the end of your rope, lying motionless and praying you wouldn't hear the footsteps of the cartel coming up behind you. At one point I didn't care if the cartel shot me or not. It didn't seem to matter anymore.

Then I had hallucinations leading me to themes of self-betrayal, "If they would just give me a sip of water before they shot me," I thought to myself. "I would be so grateful if they would give me just one drink of cool water..."

I felt I had mere moments left before everything faded to final darkness. That's when I had my biggest and final jolt of fear. I couldn't remember who I was.

"What was my name? Had I forgotten my own identity?" I thought to myself. "What about my friends? What of my family? How will I vouch for my soul if I die and I don't know who I am?"

That was the last thought I had before everything went totally dark. So, as my final act of desperation, I bellowed out my last words into a merciless desert heat, "Oh God...don't let me leave like this."

# 2.

# Fifteen Years Earlier — 2000
# The Descendants of Lorenzo De Zavala

When I was a boy, I had no direction in life. Like many teenagers, I wandered aimlessly from one day to the next, searching for anything that could be exciting even if the cause came from something of a mischievous nature. And many times it did.

I had no sense of who I was and never ever gave the future any consideration. You could say I was the typical teenager with a defiant attitude. As I got a little older, things got progressively worse.

At fifteen years old, I started to run with a group of hoodlums through the streets of San Antonio. We were always up to no good. Too often we would stay up all night long, drinking and smoking things we had no business with.

After one of those nights, I came home only to find my things packed in a backpack and sitting on the front porch. My mother had kicked me out of the house. After some harsh words, tears shed, and my mother slamming the door in my face, I picked up my backpack and walked to my cousin's house.

I never knew how important my family was until I didn't have them anymore. Sure I had my cousin's house to stay at, but it wasn't the same. To have my mother reject me, something I didn't think was possible, was too much for my mind to handle.

Two weeks before Thanksgiving in 2000, my mother came to get me and bring me back home. Needless to say, I apologized.

"It'll never happen again," I promised her, and I meant it.

I was only fifteen when I made that promise. I don't know where it came from, but I could see in her face what I told her carried a lot of weight.

▼ ▼ ▼

During the Thanksgiving holiday of 2000, we drove to my grandfather's ranch in Pleasanton. There were always plenty of things to do there if you were one of the grandkids.

I remember it specifically because that year a super cold front came in two days earlier and that's all the adults seemed to talk about.

My younger brother Tony and I didn't care about the weather, and we weren't about to spend all day and night sitting inside the house where all the grownups wouldn't shut up about the weather. Boring. So we built a campfire in the backyard. That was sort of a family tradition.

When no one was looking, Tony and I would poke at the fire with our sticks, making ourselves into annoying safety hazards.

To us, that was good entertainment. We were glad to be there. In fact, as long as we weren't sitting in some classroom at school, we were glad to be anywhere. But don't get the wrong idea, we both knew school was a necessary thing.

My "sitting in a classroom attention span" was often overshadowed by the growth hormones that young men must bear at that age. Adolescence hit me like a stick up the side of the head. Often, I found myself thinking so deeply and hard, I was convinced I must have been the smartest person in the world.

Every morning I'd look at my skinny one-hundred-pound frame in the mirror and ask, "Who are you?" as if the mirror was going to tell me my fortune. After pretending to be deep in thought, I'd stare back at my reflection and answer, "My name is Luis De Zavala. I am fifteen years old. I'm a genius and no one knows it."

You never know the importance of being humble until you are forced to look real close in that mirror like I had in front of mine one morning. "I can't go to school like this!" I said to myself in surprise. "I have a big zit growing on my nose."

It made me wonder if there was anything else right under my own nose that I couldn't see. I was learning that life was full of unforeseen problems and caveats.

My brother Tony, or Antonio as my mother sometimes screamed his name, didn't spend much time wondering about the complexities of life. He spent the majority of his time wondering what girls looked like without their clothes. I think he went into deep contemplation about that and where his next meal was coming from. Quite frankly, Tony was a bottomless pit. When it was time to eat, you best get your food quickly before Tony dove in.

During our high school years, Tony began to put on the pounds and get a little chubby. That interfered with his ability to romance the girls, so he learned to push away the doughnuts, joined the high school football team, and turned into the Mexican American version of the *Incredible Hulk*. Strong as a bull, appetite of a horse, and sometimes the thought process of a squirrel.

Despite any faults Tony had, one thing was a constant, and that was family loyalty. Since Tony was one year younger than me, you might say that we grew up going in the same direction. Every time either one of us did something important, we would always be there for the other brother.

However, there was one non-contested difference. I had always been the leader of us. Tony had always been my support. He was never motivated by any philosophical purposes or personally driven egos. He was honest to the core and always there as my biggest supporter.

It was no coincidence that over the years we both became the unwitting leaders in our generation under the De Zavala banner. It was in our blood. For those that knew us, it probably made perfect sense. After all, we learned as apprentices under the watchful eye of our grandfather, Sergio De Zavala, as was handed down to him by the great Lorenzo De Zavala, a seldom accredited figure in Texas history.

Over time, Tony and I were compelled to battle the inequities of lesser men. It was an instinct that came naturally to both of us and led us down the path to many adventures.

My brother and I both have our stories, but this one is mine. For I am the academic of the family, and I can tell my story—hopefully without distortions.

❦ ❦ ❦

The tradition of sitting around the campfire after Thanksgiving dinner didn't happen as much as we wished it did. It was a yearly problem. Of course, everybody would declare their intentions to hang out by the fire. That is until they stuffed themselves on too much turkey, dressing, and every kind of Mexican side dish possible. Within an hour, the entire family would show signs of tryptophan overdoses. The effects usually put all the weak ones under a sleeping spell, causing them to nod off in place. The rest of them just lay there like hogs in the mud.

Tony and I never could figure out why everyone stayed inside. We made the fire for them. To us, standing around the fire was the best part of Thanksgiving.

Their excuses were always the same, "We're too full to stand by the fire," followed by painful grunts and groans. In other words, everyone ate too much food and then they wimped out.

That was okay with me and Tony. We didn't want any adult supervision while we waved our fiery sticks in the air anyway. Someone might try to tell us what to do, and that would suck all the fun out of it.

I went to the main house and tried to get my fat cousin Ignacio out the door, *"Orale vato!* We got the fire going. Get off your ass and come outside."

Ignacio turned his fat head and took a shallow breath, "I ate too many *chicharrónes*. I barely can move anymore!"

What Ignacio meant was he had just polished off about ten pounds of fried pig meat. A proud accomplishment for a barbecue joint if you were selling it by the pound but risky under the "all you can eat" plan. A fat bastard like Ignacio could make the books dip into the red if you didn't supervise him.

So much for that effort. We had other cousins, but that year they were down in Port Aransas trying to catch the big fish they saw on TV.

Tony and I both had our fire sticks burning well. Then we decided to play "grab-ass" and burn one another's butts with the fiery ends. Since the non-recognized game of "grab ass" has no rules, I'm sure we looked like two near-sighted samurais, leaving streaks of burning embers in the air and quickly burning holes in one another's clothes.

"What the hell? Cut that shit out!" came that voice of commanding authority out of the darkness. It was the patron himself, our grandfather the owner of the ranch and head honcho of the De Zavala family, Papa Sergio De Zavala.

Papa Sergio was well respected by the local community as well as being deeply loved by his own family. As kids, we had always been told we were the descendants of the famous Lorenzo De Zavala, the first vice president of the Republic of Texas and one of the drafters and signers of the Texas Constitution. As young teenagers of that time, that meant very little to us.

Tony and I had always assumed we were his favorites of all the grandkids. After all, we spent more time with him than the other cousins did. But even as Papa Sergio's favorites, we knew very little about our grandfather, and now things were about to change. What he was going to tell us around the campfire would have a long and lasting effect on both of our lives—that of an unwritten code, not explainable to so many others.

"You keep acting like kids, people will keep treating you like kids," Papa Sergio warned us.

We irritated our grandfather from time to time, but we always knew he was still on our side.

Papa sat down in one of the chairs without saying another word. He stared into the burning coals and an uncomfortable silence developed among us. Those were the first signs that we were probably in trouble. Tony and I sat down, waiting and hoping that Papa Sergio would speak first.

Then Papa Sergio slowly reached into his inside coat pocket and pulled out a bottle of whiskey. After he took a snort, he noticed me watching, "You know what this is?"

"Sure, it's whiskey," I answered innocently. Then I decided it was time to get Papa all riled up by jerking his chain a little, something we all did to each other from time to time. "Can I have a drink? You know, just between us men?"

"Hell no!" Papa Sergio glanced at the house, "What the hell is wrong with you? Your mother would kill me."

Then I started to pour it on again, "You're not afraid of our mother, Papa. Just admit it, you just don't like us very much—of all the people in the world, your own grandchildren?"

Tony squinched his face to look like he was going to cry and then poured on the bullshit even thicker, "We include you in our prayers, Papa, and you don't even like us?"

"Our own grandfather," I whined.

"I think I'm going to eat a mangy opossum and die!" Tony topped off his act.

It didn't take long before Papa had enough of our comedy routine, "Both of you got shit for brains, you know that? What do you two ever expect to be in life anyway?"

Tony was first, "I'm going to become a linebacker for the *Dallas Cowboys*."

Papa Sergio leaned in towards Tony, "That is what the *gringos* would call a 'lofty goal.' But you could do it."

Then Papa looked at me, "What about you, troublemaker?" Papa asked.

"I'm going to search for buried treasure," I told Papa, "and when I find my chest full of gold I'll have enough money to buy my own whiskey."

"Until that time comes, you stay away from this panther piss," Papa Sergio commanded. "It'll cloud your mind, make you take a crooked trail."

Tony just couldn't keep his mouth shut, "I think it's too late, Papa. I drank enough to drown a horse."

"Tony!" I tried to make it obvious for him to shut up.

It was too late. Tony confessed our sins before I could stop him, "Luis here? He's drunk enough to drown two horses."

Like I said before, sometimes Tony had the thinking process of a squirrel. So I took my fiery stick and whopped him along the shoulder of his thick coat. He didn't feel a thing through that thick coat. Then both of us drew back our sticks, ready for a fight.

"Cut that shit out!" Papa Sergio ordered.

"He sold me out! He does that all the time," I protested.

"Yeah, well, there's worse things," Papa concluded.

After things calmed down and we re-took our seats, I felt compelled to ask, "How old were you when you had your first drink?"

"I was old enough."

"Come on, Papa...your first serious drink of whiskey?" I asked again.

Papa Sergio finally looked me in the eyes, "About your age, and it was Tequila."

"Did you have visions?" I asked Papa.

I could tell by the bad look on his face, I had asked the wrong question. "Visions? Only a dumb *gringo* would have visions over something so stupid. You want a vision, eat some peyote, or better yet, let Tony hit you on the head with that stick of his. Maybe you'll get visions."

Then Tony pleaded for me, "I don't think he was serious about having the visions, Papa."

That was one of the few times my grandfather ever barked at me for reasons unknown. I immediately dismissed it because I could sense there was something on his mind, but to a grandson that idolized his grandfather, it still hurt a little.

Papa quickly glanced into the darkness and back to the fire. It confused us for a moment. He acted like someone might sneak up from behind or something, or maybe eavesdrop on his conversation. We didn't know, but whatever Papa had on his mind, he wasn't about to tell us until he was good and ready.

It was only when he looked into the coals of the fire for a few minutes did he seem to relax. And you could tell Papa Sergio was remembering things. Perhaps from the old days.

"I only got seven years of school when my father took me out to work. For the next three years, I grazed over three-thousand Spanish goats, alone."

"That's a bunch of goats," Tony commented.

Papa Sergio looked at me, "What have you done, Luis? What have you done to earn that drink?"

Papa Sergio had made his point clear, and I felt slightly ashamed. In fact, I wasn't qualified.

My own grandfather had instantly placed everything into perspective. So, I gave him a glimpse of my intentions, "One day I will. One of these days I'll do something great. Maybe I can make you proud of me then."

"I am proud of you now, both of you. And I have no doubt you will make me proud in the future. You will become like your great-great-grandfather, an honorable and well-respected man, Lorenzo De Zavala."

"What about our grandfather, the Great Sergio?" Tony asked.

Sergio paused. There was something about the question that hit a nerve with Papa. He gave Tony the intimidating stare and the somber tone, "All I had ever been was a goat herder. *Vaquero de calida!*"

"What about World War II?" I asked in confusion. "Is it true you shot Adolf Hitler in the ass?"

Papa Sergio started to laugh, "Well if it was, I would be a hero, wouldn't I?"

Tony started to join in on the laugh, "That would be something. We could tell everyone!"

Papa Sergio sat up straight and took the bottle out of his pocket. "I'll drink to that," then turned it up for a drink. As soon as he finished his sip, he offered the bottle to me. "Don't tell your mother," he warned me.

Tony and I both got a swig of whiskey. Not enough to feel any effects, but the toast wasn't about getting drunk anyway. It was about continuing the tradition of De Zavala men around the campfire. We were always ready to hang with our grandfather. He was the only significant male figure we had.

Then Papa began to talk about the future, "I'm glad you boys are both here. You are the only real men left in the family, and I need to tell you some things. Very important things."

"Sure, Papa Sergio," I said.

This kind of serious conversation didn't happen very often with Tony and me. At the time, everyone still considered us children, aimlessly wandering with no care in the world.

What Papa Sergio was about to tell us that night was going to change the trajectory of our futures. He would plant the seeds of what would turn us into better men. We would travel on a long and far adventure to reach the end.

Papa Sergio looked us straight in the eyes and things got very serious.

"I'm seventy-eight years old, and I don't know how long I've got left on this earth. When I die, there might be fighting over what to do with the ranch. I think all my children will agree to sell the ranch and split the money three ways. One-third will go to your mother Anna, one-third to your Aunt Monica, and the remainder to your Aunt Evangelina. It was my bad luck I had all girls. I had no sons. Your grandmother... she did her best."

"No more De Zavala ranch? Where would build the family fire?" Tony asked.

I couldn't believe what I was hearing, "They wouldn't do that! Would they? Sell the ranch?"

"I know my girls," Sergio said. "Not one of them has the money to buy out the other two sisters, so they will have to agree to sell the ranch and divide the money."

I looked into the fire and started to think, "I can't imagine no more ranch...and you not being here?"

"Everyone will die," Sergio continued. "You know the three shipping containers that I covered with dirt?"

"The ones with those huge locks?" Tony asked.

"Sure we do," I acknowledged. "How long have they been buried?"

Sergio continued, "Years. Each container has things I am leaving to you and all the other grandchildren. This is your inheritance. My daughters may sell the ranch, but it is in my will that each individual container goes to the grandchildren of each family. Your container is in the middle, but don't get sneaky. You can't break the lock of the container until I am dead."

"What's in it?" Tony asked innocently.

"Only things a man would like," Papa Sergio continued. "The uniform I wore in the army and other army things. Fishing things, hunting things...old saddles, old pictures...some artifacts. You know, interesting things."

Tony asked, "What do you leave a person like Ignacio?"

"A frying pan, a cookbook, and a hundred pounds of jerky made from a mule that I shot in the head. You don't worry about Ignacio."

"You know?" I spoke without thinking, "Finding that buried treasure of gold would come in handy right about now. I could buy the ranch and keep it in the family."

Tony raised his head, "Yeah. I think I'll buy some shovels tomorrow, and we can start digging for gold."

Papa Sergio raised his hand, "Before you get carried away with tales of lost treasures, I got to tell you some things. Riches can lead a man into deep sin, and the corruption that follows can lead to your destruction. There is always a price to pay. Take the wrong step, and you could lose your life. Chase the luster of the gold, and you could lose your soul."

Our grandfather was an expert at dangling the carrot in front of our noses to make us walk a little further. We were hooked the minute he recited that Del Rancho philosophy, something we never heard before or since.

"How do you know? Were you a treasure hunter?" I asked.

"When I was young, I was what you might call a prospector. There was a lot of prospecting in those days, but eventually I stopped looking."

"Did you ever find anything?" Tony asked.

Sergio waved his hands back and forth, "That's not important. Let me tell you a story. A true story."

# 3.

## The Golden Aztec Eagle Warriors
## (The Gringo and the Vaquero)

Papa Sergio took a big swallow from his whiskey bottle and began his story. We were already on the edge of our seats.

"I knew two men that lived in Bandera. One was a *gringo*. He was a dentist and had lots of money. The other was a Mexican *vaquero* and was well known to all the local ranches. They were good friends and did many things together. The *vaquero* and the *gringo* liked to hunt deer together, so every winter the *gringo* and the *vaquero* would fly to Mexico in the small airplane that the *gringo* owned.

Every hunt was successful. The kills were donated to the local villagers that hosted them, and everyone was happy.

During the return of one of their hunts in Mexico, they had plane trouble and were forced to land in the mountains. After they fixed the plane, they cleared a runway to take off again. But while they were clearing the path, they stumbled upon a cave.

When they entered the cave, they found an old Aztec sacrificial chamber."

I raised my hand and asked, "How did they know it was Aztec?"

"Because there were fifty golden statues of Aztec Eagle Warriors, twenty-five on each side of the walls of the cave. All of them three feet tall.

"Gold?" Tony asked. "Real gold?"

Papa Sergio looked at Tony and then at me. We didn't know it, but he had us right where he wanted. He watched us closely, trying to see if we were going to be motivated by the tales of riches or something else.

I'm easily enthralled with a story like Papa's. My imagination had me standing in that cave and looking at those golden statues. The more intense the story became, the deeper my mind traveled back in time. The beating of my own heart, which became the echoing drumbeats of the Aztecs, long gone.

"Yes, gold," Papa told us. "But that's not the end of the story: At the far side of the cave there was an altar made of stone. It was a sacrificial chamber from ancient times. Above the altar was a small opening to the sky, sometimes allowing sunlight to come in.

The *vaquero* climbed onto the altar and tried to see out the opening, but the electricity that was in the walls of the cave was crawling all over his body making him feel like he was covered in ants. His hair would stand straight out, and lightning would crackle in the air."

"Did they take one of the statues with them?" I asked.

"No. It was a small plane and just one Eagle Warrior was too heavy. The *gringo* and *vaquero* marked the spot on the map and flew back to Bandera.

The next week, the *gringo* flew back to the cave, alone. The *vaquero* waited at the *gringo's* ranch landing strip. The plan was for the *gringo* to fly back to the cave, take one Eagle Warrior, and fly back to the *gringo's* ranch.

There was enough gold in one Eagle Warrior to make both of them wealthy. That's all they needed. Besides, the small airplane would not be able to carry more than one."

Papa Sergio stopped for a second to take a sip from his whiskey bottle then continued with his story. "The *vaquero* waited for his *gringo* friend until it became dark, but he would never leave.

Later in the night, he watched the lights of a small plane come over the horizon and approach the landing strip. Slowly the small plane floated to the ground, when something went terribly wrong and the plane crashed. There was a ball of fire, a mangled wreck that set the cedar trees and grass on fire. All was destroyed. The *vaquero's* hopes of becoming a wealthy man had vanished, and he had witnessed his friend die before his very eyes.

When the sheriff and the fire department came, the deputies asked the *vaquero* if he had searched the wreckage. The *vaquero* told them, "No. The pilot was my good friend." He could not bear the thought of seeing his friend in such a mangled and disfigured condition.

The fire department and other authorities never found anything that resembled the Eagle Warrior, but it didn't matter. The *vaquero's* heart was saddened after he witnessed his friend's terrible death. He was no longer interested in gold or other treasures, so he moved away, that he might forget."

I could almost feel the heat from the fire. The biggest impact up until that point was the crash of the airplane. This was ntot a story with a happy ending. Knowing what the *vaquero* experienced by watching his friend's death had to be tough.

"Nobody found anything?" Tony asked.

Papa Sergio shook his head, "No. Nothing."

"That must have been hard for him...his friend dying right there in front of him?" Then I looked up at Papa, "Is that the end of the story?"

"No," Papa Sergio told us. "There is one more part to the story. The most important part. A lesson you should both learn."

We were eagerly awaiting.

All of a sudden, my mother Anna walked out of that dark spot between the house and the fire. She snuck up on all of us, completely catching us off guard. How could she do that? What stealth he had.

"Got any room for a girl around this fire?" Mom asked. "What are you men talking about anyway?"

"Things," Papa said reluctantly.

Then there was Tony. He couldn't keep anything confidential among us guys, "We're talking about treasure hunting."

Mom faked being surprised, "Ah! Buried treasure! That's inter-esting. Let me take a wild guess," then looked at Papa, "would the story be about a *gringo* and a *vaquero*?"

"You know about those guys?" Tony asked.

"Since way before you were born," Mom rattled on. "Two friends chasing a dream. One of them gets killed in an airplane crash, then the *vaquero* makes a map?"

Papa Sergio interrupted her by growling like a dog, "You come all the way out here to shoot me in the ass?"

I looked at Mom and asked innocently, "Mom, you don't believe the story?"

"Well, I believe there was a *gringo* and a *vaquero*...at least." She laughed at her own answer.

Papa Sergio looked her in the eyes and gave the angry dog growl again.

Mom got the message, "Boy! It sure is cold out here. I think I'll go back inside where it's warm," looking at Sergio, "and safer."

"Sorry to see you leave," Papa said sarcastically.

"I'm sure you are. That's okay, this is a man's fire. No girls allowed I supposed. It wouldn't be the first time." After she stood up, she leaned in on Papa Sergio and told him out of the corner of her mouth, "If you give them a drink of that Thanksgiving whiskey, you and I are going to have some words. You *sabe*, mister treasure hunter?"

"Are you going to leave us alone?" Papa pleaded with her.

"Yes, yes, I'm going." Then Mom gave Papa a quick hug and a kiss on the cheek. "Happy Thanksgiving, Papa."

She faded back into the darkness from whence she came. Everyone's dignity still intact.

I was thinking to myself that only a professional mother could do something like that. She had caused damage, set the record straight, given a strict warning, and repaired the damage before she left the crime scene, all under five minutes. I've never been able to do something like that.

As soon she left the light of the campfire, we got back down to business.

When Mom reached the door of the house, Tony spoke up, "Then what happened?"

Papa leaned in and started where he left off.

"The *vaquero* lived in North Texas for many years and never told anyone what had happened. Then one day he was reading the newspaper and noticed a very particular advertisement at the back of the paper. It was an ad looking for investors to help start a gold mine in Mexico. The *vaquero* called them and the following day they had a meeting.

The two men that came to see the *vaquero* were both *gringos*. Their names were Marvin and Ronny, and they were also from the Bandera area. The *vaquero* asked if they knew the dentist and they didn't, but they did remember the airplane crash as small boys. That was big news in those days and everyone remembered."

I stopped Papa to make sure I had the story right, "Wait a minute, Papa. Let me get this straight. The *vaquero's gringo* friend was from Bandera...and so were Marvin and Ronny? Was that coincidence?"

"Maybe. Yes? I don't know."

"Tell us more, Papa," insisted Tony.

"The *vaquero* decided to tell them his story of his *gringo* friend that was killed in the crash, the cave, the golden Eagle Warriors, and how tragedy had befallen them.

The *vaquero* even showed them the map he had made over forty years before. Marvin and Ronny soon forgot about their gold mining project and changed their plans. They decided to search for the cave of the golden Eagle Warriors instead.

When they tried to get the *vaquero* to go with them to Mexico, the *vaquero* declined the offer. He told them that all his desires to dig for treasures and chase golden statues had vanished.

I knew these *gringos,* not very well, but still I knew them. They were known to be less than honest men."

"The *vaquero* sold them the map?" I guessed.

"No, he gave it to them," Papa Sergio continued, "and then they instantly forgot everything about their own gold mine."

"So did they find it?" Tony asked.

"There's more. They bought five horses and hired a guide. The guide took them through the mountains and to the right location where they could see the entrance to the cave. There was a fence between them and the cave, and the guide absolutely refused to cross it until they all got permission from the owner. The next day, they traveled to see the owner of that ranch to get permission.

The owner of the ranch told them that he had no such cave and refused to let them on his ranch.

In most cases that would have been the end of the quest, but the two *gringos* had spent the majority of their money on the five horses and the time and expenses it took to get there. They felt they had no choice but to cross the fence the next day—to trespass.

That night before they were to cross, there was a bad argument between Marvin and his friend Ronny. Marvin wanted to melt the gold statues down before they crossed back into the United States, and Ronny insisted on crossing the border with the statues intact. This argument divided them terribly, and they almost got into a fight with each other.

That night a terrible thunderstorm hit their camp. The violent winds destroyed much of their equipment. Lightning struck the ground all around them, and two of the horses pulled loose and ran into the canyons.

It took them most of the next day to find their horses and repair their camp. And still, they were two friends divided.

At the end of the same day, a small boy rode up on a burro as fast as he could. He had a message for Marvin. He said, "Your son has been shot in San Antonio. He barely lives. Please come home quick."

Without hesitation, Marvin and Ronny gathered what they could and left for the United States. When they crossed into Del Rio, both of them made telephone calls to their homes. Marvin's son had died at the hospital.

Then there was more bad news. Ronny learned from his phone call that doctors had amputated both of his oldest son's legs the night before. He had gangrene from diabetes. Before he would reach the hospital in San Antonio, Ronny's son would also die.

I went to the funeral for Marvin's son. It was a very sad day. Marvin was never the same after his son's death."

"Two sons dead before they could get back home? Did Marvin and Ronny ever make friends again?" I asked.

"No, they didn't," Papa Sergio continued. "They never saw each other again, and they lost their desire for riches."

Papa stopped talking and we all looked into the coals of the fire for a few minutes. Somewhere inside of me I wanted this sad story to be true, but my own mother put doubt in my head, and I wondered about it.

The fact was that Papa Sergio knew too many details about the story for it to not be true. That's how I justified it.

"Papa," I probed, "things were going so well for them. Sounds like they planned for everything. How did things go so wrong?"

That was the question Papa Sergio was there for and Papa planned it that way. From that point forward, he was going to push and entice Tony and me to think for ourselves and come to the same moral conclusion when it came to man's quest for treasures. It was to be the critical warning we both needed to hear.

"You remember the cave they went into?" Papa continued, "Again, I tell you. It was an ancient Aztec sacrificial chamber, and if it wasn't Aztec, then it was like the Aztecs or maybe the Mayans. Do you know what they did on that altar?"

"That's where they all got together and ate dinner," Tony tried to answer.

Papa scoffed at him, "No!"

Then it was my turn for the smart-ass approach, "They played cards?"

"I have serious doubts my grandsons will amount to anything." He looked up into the dark sky and held out his hands to the heavens, as if he was asking for forgiveness, "Oh God, forgive me! You see what I have to work with."

"Or maybe—" I interrupted and held his attention for a moment, "people were sacrificed there on that altar."

"Oh yeah?" Tony inquired, "How many people do you figure died there?"

Papa pointed up to the sky, "Thousands. Put the clues together and think. Electricity in the walls? A sacrificial altar? This was a place of great importance. Thousands of people died there on that very altar. Now, where did their souls go?"

"Hundreds of years ago?" Tony asked and thought about it.

"Yes," Papa continued. "You tell me. Were their souls left simply to linger in that very exact spot? Where do you think they went?"

"They never left. That's what I think," I said out loud. "The spirits are protecting the gold...or the chamber. Every time someone tries to take something, something bad seems to happen." I looked into Papa's eyes to see if I was right, "That cave is still haunted. Isn't it?"

"Luis is right. Ghosts never get too old or retire from the ghost business," Tony said. "They'll be there forever. The *gringo* and the *vaquero* should have never gone back to the cave the second time."

"Yeah but, how would they know it was cursed?" I asked.

Then Papa gave his conclusion, "It doesn't matter whether they knew it or not. They were driven by one of the most destructive sins of man, greed. Not once did they enter these sacred sites with pure intentions or humble hearts. Not once did they pray to God or pay homage to the souls that stood watch. All across the world in many cultures, priests and shamans will make offerings to their gods before entering their most holy sites...being respectful and asking permission. Remember these things I tell you. Riches are not the most important things in this world."

"Money can't buy happiness," I told everyone.

Papa Sergio's lessons were clear. Of course, at our age it took a whole storybook chapter to make sure we remembered it. Number one was to never give in to the sin of greed. Number two was to never enter a sacred site without a pure heart and before paying homage to the ones that perished there.

It would take ten full years of mental preparation before I saw these morals come into play. During that time, you might say I grew up and set some goals in my life.

♦ ♦ ♦

Of all the stories Papa Sergio told us, Tony and I would remember one more than any other. It was Papa's prediction that when he died the ranch would be sold off. It was a future problem, yes, but it was almost as haunting. Perhaps instilled into our heads so that we wouldn't be so devastated when the time came.

Tony and I couldn't fathom the ranch being gone. It had always been the base camp of the De Zavalas. The center of countless family gatherings, our home away from home. Despite all the good intentions in the world, it all came down to money. The fact was that the ranch was worth ten times more than when it was originally bought. All of Papa's daughters, including my own mother, wouldn't have enough money to buy the other two out, nor would they have any interest in taking it over. No one in the age of calculus and algorithms wanted to work hard and be a rancher.

Then time passed. After four years at the University of Texas in San Antonio, I was about to receive my degree in archeology and I didn't have a job, yet. I was spending most of my time as an amateur treasure hunter on a constant chase to validate and secure history. And I did it with a humble heart, as taught to me by my grandfather, Sergio De Zavala.

# 4.

## Twelve Years Later — 2012
## The Lost Spanish Cache on the Old Spanish Trail

My brother was in his room going through his personal things with a fine-toothed comb and packing his bags. Tony had joined the U.S. Army and was on the delayed enlistment program. In six months he had to report for duty. All those muscles he had been building gave him the idea that he could be more than he already was, so he decided to put it to the test.

The army gave him an IQ test, but evidently they have no problem training squirrels to throw hand grenades and fire missiles like they were bottle rockets.

About the same time, I was sitting with my mother at her kitchen table and looking at my diploma from the University of Texas. The dean handed it to me during the graduation ceremony the night before. I knew Mom was proud of me, but quite frankly I had no idea what I was going to do next.

"A degree in Archeology?" I looked up at my mother, "What am I going to do with this...*chingadera*?"

"You better find a job, *hijo*," she said while sipping her coffee. "In six months you're going to be married. You need to be working... keep that new bride of yours happy."

Mom tried to hide her grin behind the coffee cup, but there was a running joke behind that grin. Although I tried to dare her with my hard stares, she couldn't hold it together any longer and started to chuckle.

My doubts and worries about getting married to this girl by the name of Amelia were obvious to everyone in the family. Everyone seemed mildly alarmed except for me. As far as I knew, these were minor relationship kinks. Normal things that had to be worked out in a relationship. My own mother had more fun watching me struggle than anyone in the family. Looking back, I had to admit it was kind of funny, but not at the time.

Amelia was as honest and faithful as any man would want, but she was also needy, a whiner of the highest order, and ridiculously afraid of anything that didn't come from Walmart.

It was impossible to take her hunting or fishing. She complained about mosquitoes, fishing worms, snakes, coyotes, *chupacabras*, and of all things, getting dirty from sitting on the ground. There was no light at the end of her tunnel. My mother loved her, but in private settings, Amelia was often made fun of by the rest of my family.

So, there my mother was rubbing it in, snickering and trying to hide behind that stupid-looking cup of coffee.

I leaned slightly over the table, "Go ahead and laugh. I don't think that's funny at all. She's going to be your daughter-in-law one day."

The phone rang, and Mom picked it up, "This is the De Zavala's house for disturbed children! Can I help you?" Mom's expression changed, "Oh, hi Cade. Yes, he's right here...I will. Tell Theresa hello for me."

I took the phone from her and within a minute the atmosphere instantly changed. The man on the other side of the phone was a long-time friend of the family, Cade Ferguson.

When I barged into Tony's room, he was flexing his muscles in front of a full-sized mirror. *"Oye, Fabio!* Put on a shirt. We got a mission."

Within minutes, we were burning up the road like outlaws running from the cops, and there was a good reason for it.

♦ ♦ ♦

Cade Ferguson and his wife, Theresa, were not only great friends, but they were also arrowhead diggers like us and a valuable source to conspire with because of one big advantage, Cade was in the excavation business. His company was always digging up some artifact somewhere. And when he did, he always gave me a call. Over the years we spent a lot of time together either organizing archaeological digs or actually digging the sites.

We were considered amateur archaeologists, and we all belonged to a group called the Texas Artifacts Diggers. We dug at sites where native Indians or historical sites were once located to sift the dirt and recover the artifacts. We didn't dig for any government entity or big university. We dug for ourselves, collecting, recording, and sometimes trading with each other what we recovered. Everyone in our digging group had some kind of artifact collection, but arrowheads were the majority of the finds.

Early on, we made it a point that the landowners and the dig sites were to be treated with respect. We never allowed anyone to desecrate these dig sites. Most importantly, no human remains were ever allowed to be removed from their original positions. It was this code of ethics that we established early in our group's formation.

♦ ♦ ♦

Timing became everything. Cade got a tip from one of his construction crews that one of his road graders uncovered pieces of what looked like a Spanish wooden keg while cutting a new road across Salado Creek. The location was exactly where the Old Spanish Trail crossed Salado Creek, and we both knew what that meant. One of the legends of a lost Spanish cache was probably true.

In the 1780s, Spanish *Conquistadors* buried a cache of wooden kegs filled with gold, golden figurines, and priceless gems on the banks of the Salado Creek while they were being harassed by Indians. Everyone in the Spanish detail was either killed or separated from the incident for one reason or another. No one ever came back to recover it.

Treasure hunters had been looking for this cache for the last three-hundred years, but so much time had elapsed that the story became more myth than fact.

All I could think of on the way to the site was, "If we didn't do this right the first time, there would be no second chance."

There was a good reason for our hasty and yet apprehensive approach to this find. It was because of one man, my nemesis by the name of Professor Andrew Wilson, the Director of Archeology for the State of Texas. Wilson had single-handedly caused inconveniences and hardships for every amateur arrowhead collector in the state of Texas. When Andrew Wilson got involved, everything became uncontrollably complicated and expensive.

State law required that all construction companies halt work and notify Wilson's office when they found artifacts. Wilson's department would legally take total control of the site and document the findings.

The problem was what I noticed over a period of time. Some artifacts disappeared. I've never been able to prove it, but I've always suspected that these items ended up on the black market, not in the museum where they belonged.

That's why I had to get to the discovery site before Wilson did.

I was driving my pickup as fast as I could without being pulled over. We had about an hour of daylight left and to make matters worse, there was a thunderstorm to the north of San Antonio. They were dark and looked heavy with rain. Flooding was a real possibility, and lightning was crawling all over the skies.

"Okay, Luis. You want to tell me what we're doing?" Tony asked.

"Cade called the house," I shouted over the road noise. "He got a call from one of his construction workers about some things that were dug up by accident on the banks of the Salado. You know what that means?"

Tony didn't have a clue, "No! What?"

Asking Tony these kinds of questions was close to useless, "I think they found the lost Spanish cache, remember?"

"No! I don't." He started to put on his seatbelt, "Say homie, why you driving so fast? You're scaring the shit out of me."

"Because the site was roped off late this afternoon, after they called the state," I tried to explain to him. "Wilson is going to be there tomorrow morning and claim it for himself. I just know it."

This was an old reoccurring problem to Tony. He was tired of hearing about the friction between me and Professor Wilson. Tony shook his head, "Don't you mean claim it for the state? He is the government authority, you know?"

"He steals from dig sites where he's not invited," I loudly clarified. "Whose side are you on anyway?"

"I'm on your side, Luis. I don't like the guy any more than you do, but you got to give it a rest. It's going to drive you crazy."

"I know. I know," I told him. "Look, Tony, Wilson is going to get there no matter what we do, but if we can dig it out first and catalog it before he gets there, then he'll be less likely to steal anything."

Tony looked at me with a serious gaze, "If it was roped off for Wilson, then it already belongs to the state and we'll be the ones breaking the law. How do you feel about doing time for some unknown antiquities law?"

That had turned into a philosophical question, and I had to stand up for what I believed about archeology, "I think it would be worth it."

Tony stared at me. I knew he remembered what our Papa Sergio told us years before, "Yeah. Probably so. I'm sure the Spanish angels will be relieved when they see their golden chest of trinkets pulled out of the ground."

"They're in kegs. Wooden kegs."

Tony looked out his window and saw the storm shoot lightning across the sky. It looked bad. *Viene una gran tormenta, Primo.* It looks like a turd floater."

Tony was right. Those clouds were dark and destructive looking.

I drove between two safety cones and into the construction site, which was the road that they were grading. Not to attract any unneeded attention, I also turned off my lights and slowed down considerably so we wouldn't kick up too much dust.

The key to our entire approach was to keep a low profile, enough that even the neighborhood watch wouldn't be alarmed by our presence. These road construction sites were notorious for equipment thefts, and we didn't want anyone calling the police on us.

We followed the graded road all the way to Salado Creek and I parked the truck in the middle of all the other construction equipment, hoping it would blend in.

The construction company was going to build a bridge over the Salado Creek. That's when they excavated through the creek bank and accidentally unearthed the Spanish artifacts.

As we got out of the truck, we noticed two things: The first was that storm. It was a big mother. The second thing we noticed was someone's private backyard party about five hundred yards to the left of us, downstream. The bright lights and music were coming from a rich neighborhood, and they were just getting started.

I handed Tony a flashlight and a pick. I grabbed a shovel then looked in the direction of the party, "Looks like someone is having fun."

"Yeah...and we should be there with them, sucking down some cold ones," Tony mildly complained.

I didn't blame Tony for being a little tired of these missions I volunteered him for. Every single time I had one, I called him for help. But the older he got, the less he wanted to go.

We walked down to the water and found the cache area on the right side of the road, up against the east bank. It was completely roped off with construction tape and red construction fencing, so we went over the fence and up to the riverbank where it looked slightly disturbed. Then it became obvious.

"This has to be the place," I told Tony.

The buried cache was strategically located in the wall of the creek bank and directly under a rock overhang. That came in handy because when we started to dig, it started to rain, and rain hard it did.

Finding and uncovering the cache was the easy part. The Spaniards dug a big hole into the east bank of the Salado, placed the kegs inside, and then filled in the cavities with various kinds of debris. All the wooden kegs were stacked on top of each other.

The entrance was sealed with what looked like an adobe mixture made from mud and rocks they got from the creek. The Spaniards built and disguised the entrance so that no person would have a clue as to the buried treasure in the area. And for over three hundred years it worked.

The high winds, blowing rains, and lightning had become too threatening for Tony to ignore anymore, "Holy shit, *Primo!* Look at the creek. It turned into a river!"

He was right. The Salado Creek had turned into a river in flood stage.

"Let's finish up and get the hell out of here!" I yelled at Tony.

"The sooner the better," Tony said. "If the water rises another three feet, we'll be up this creek without a paddle."

Very carefully, we uncovered nine wooden kegs but never removed them from their original positions. Only one of them was damaged by the grader. Upon a closer look at the damaged keg, we uncovered a treasure hunter's dream—a variety of jewelry made with gold or silver and emeralds embedded into the jewelry. There were silver coins, gold coins, and gold chains all spilling out from that hole in the keg. It was the biggest find I had seen or witnessed anywhere or anytime.

One particular large medallion made of gold had a stamp on the back. It was the Royal Crest of the Spanish monarch, King Charles III. Whomever the medallion was meant to go to was very important at the time, but unfortunately for its destination, it never arrived.

"Hello over there!" shouted a voice from the other side of the river.

We turned out our light, for all the good it did. There was enough lightning crawling through the sky, you really didn't need a light. Whomever it was, we were discovered. Tony and I tried to make out who they were and what they were saying, but with all the noise from the storm, it was difficult.

What we could see was that there were three men standing outside of their Humvee, looking straight at us. Then the head person yelled at us again, "Hello there! Are you alright? You know you're on a state archaeological site?"

Now I knew the voice. It was Andrew Wilson from the Texas Archaeological Department. It looked like he wasn't going to wait till morning. He had to see the site immediately. Probably because he also knew the story of the Spanish cache and he knew of people like me.

"It's Wilson, Tony."

"Professor Wilson?" he asked, alarmed at the discovery. "Damn, *Primo*. I can't get arrested and go to jail. The army won't take me if I do."

Tony was ready to bolt.

"It's not going to come to that, brother. I won't let it," I promised, trying to assure him.

Then Wilson yelled again, "Luis De Zavala? Is that you over there?"

"Don't say a word!" I told Tony, "I'm willing to bet he can't identify us yet. Not really."

Tony became irate with my conclusion, "What are you talking about, *Primo*? He just called you by name. Are you out of your fucking mind?"

"There's too much dark and rain between us and him," I tried to say with confidence, "He's guessing."

"That's a pretty good guess, I'd say. I'm out of here."

We picked up our tools and headed towards the cut in the bank that led to the graded road, but two people with flashlights were coming down towards us. Now we were truly up a creek. We had foes on all sides that wanted to arrest us and a storm doing its best to demoralize us.

"I'm going to have your ass if that's you, De Zavala," Wilson yelled for the last time.

"Downriver?" asked Tony.

"Down the river, and ditch the tools."

We threw the shovel, pick, and flashlights into the water. It was a replaceable loss. Then we jumped into the water.

Let me tell you something about raging floodwaters brought in by a thunderstorm from the north. It was cold, swift, and in the dark. It was a treacherous bastard. For as short of a time as we were in there, it kicked our asses, banging us into trees and rocks, sucking our bodies underwater before we could get a breath of air.

This was not like tubing down the Guadalupe with a beer in your hand. It was dark as hell, and you couldn't see what was coming until it hit you right in the face.

Somehow, Tony and I managed to get out and crawl out onto the east side of the creek, directly under that party we saw earlier. All the people at the party had gone inside, and a number of them were watching out the glass windows and patio doors.

I hated to do it, but we had no choice but to walk through their yard while the storm was still tearing shit up. When we did, it caused quite a stir among the people looking out the patio windows. Our clothes were barely hanging on and we were covered with mud. Concerned drunks swarmed out the doors, even in the middle of the storm. They were evidently compelled to find out what was going on.

The owner shouted, "Oh my god! Are you guys alright?"

"Yeah. We're okay," I tried to assure them.

"Come in out of the rain," the owner told us as he ushered us under a large patio covering.

"What were you doing down there?" asked the first drunk.

I didn't know exactly what to say.

A moment of silence passed, then Tony stepped up and knocked it out of the ballpark. "We were training for the 2014 Summer Olympics...the whitewater canoe race in Bogotá. Everything was fine until that storm came out of nowhere and wrapped our canoe around a tree."

The second drunk, being drunker than the others, said, "Ah, man! What a bummer!"

"You're an Olympic athlete?" asked the first drunk.

"Yeah," said my brother that was suddenly full of shit. "You might have seen us on TV. We made the finals at the Crab City canoe trials in 2008?"

"I think I saw you on TV," said the second drunk. "I remember that. That was a hell of a race."

There was no such thing as the Crab City canoe race. Tony just made it up because he thought all the drunks would buy it. They did. Hook, line, and sinker.

"I'm sorry to hear you lost everything. Can we take you anywhere?" asked the owner.

"No. We'll be fine," I told them. "My truck is right around the corner."

I was as nervous as a cat and wanted to get out of there before Wilson had the chance of finding us. But before we went through the owner's gate, the Second Drunk gave us four cold beers and a plate of hot wings. Bravo, Tony my brother.

As we left, I could hear the First Drunk ask the Second Drunk, "Where's Crab City? I've never heard of it."

▼ ▼ ▼

The next day Wilson had his crews recover the Spanish kegs and take them to a local government building. This became big news across the city. The find was the first story on the local news stations, so Wilson decided to hold his own press conference. I caught the news highlights on TV and decided I had to be there for that conference. I left Tony at home.

There were about one hundred people attending the press conference, mostly reporters.

Wilson walked out to the podium along with four other accredited archaeologists, all from the local universities.

I tried not to, but I despised these people. I was not part of their group. Sure, I had my own four-year degree in the field, but nobody offered me a job in the field when I graduated. I was digging for myself.

In fact, I had been at odds with my professors and the academic world since I was a freshman in college. I started to cause a rift in the teacher/student relationship when I saw the lack of reverence for some of the archaeological digs on sacred sites. I became the square peg in a round peg world.

Then as my education progressed, things got worse. This group of intellects would take credit for any discoveries, publish them in archaeological journals, and then write policy for the state concerning antiquity law. Nobody else's opinion mattered.

Wilson was slightly different. I knew deep down inside that he probably reported less than he found, taking some artifacts for himself and putting them on the black market, but I was never able to prove it. To me, he was a real tomb raider, and yet the *cabron* was in charge of for the whole State of Texas.

Wilson lightly tapped on the microphone to see if it was on, "Good evening, ladies and gentlemen. I am proud to announce to everyone the discovery and recovery of a lost Spanish cache from the 1700s. I won't give the exact location, but I will tell you this much – this cache contained a variety of gold and precious jewelry pieces unlike we have ever seen before. In all, we recovered a total of eight wooden kegs that were used..."

"What happened to the ninth keg?" I shouted over Wilson.

Everyone turned and looked at me. I had stepped right in the middle of it.

"I beg your pardon?" Wilson blindly asked before he saw my face.

"I said, what happened to the ninth keg? There were nine kegs. What happened to the ninth?" And then I stood there, waiting for it to come.

As soon as Wilson recognized me, he shouted to the park police that were standing on the side, "Officers, arrest that man. We have an arrest warrant for his trespassing on an archaeological site!"

Oh, well. They arrested me and put me in jail. Not a good place to be. There would be lots of explaining over this one.

# 5.

# My Gringo Friends

Jail is a great place to visit if you're a homeless psychopath in desperate need of human touch. It houses a variety of interesting characters from all walks of life. There are exceptions of course, but for the majority of the inmates, they were generally lacking in social skills.

It wasn't uncommon for any inmate to invite himself right into the middle of your business while you were not expecting it and certainly without your permission.

One man who was riding the meth train sat next to me and started telling me his life story without any commercial breaks. When I finally got away from him, the cell bully insisted on knowing my name. He left me alone after I told him my name was Speedy Gonzalez.

"You sleep on your back or stomach?" was my first alarming question. It was from a man with a divergent gaze. Somebody hit this guy in the head with a brick, and he lived to see the world on two screens. You couldn't tell where he was looking, the ceiling or the floor.

Then when I thought things were finally calming down, here came the question of the day, "You like to give it—or take it?" said the man with three green teeth.

I don't remember seeing any of these guys in church. In their early days I'm sure their mothers were constantly on their asses about going to confession, but you know, a plethora of sins to forgive takes time. Eventually Sunday comes around and the priest needs to get back to his everyday work.

With all the hollering and yelling going on twenty-four hours a day, sleep was impossible. The food was legally edible, but that was it.

Jail guards wouldn't help you with anything unless you were on fire. I think they preferred a good steady day of disorganization and chaos for a routine, otherwise they'd never know what to do with themselves.

♦ ♦ ♦

Early the next morning, the guards called my name. I was sure glad too. On that long walk down the hallway, I heard one of the inmates yell, "There goes Speedy Gonzales!"

"Fastest rat in the house!" yelled a second.

I was ready to get out of the Bexar County Jail before I contracted something that the doctors couldn't cure. My only question as I walked through the last locked door was, "Who's bailing me out?"

The second I walked through the doors I saw Amelia waiting for me in the visitor's lobby. You'll learn to appreciate someone like Amelia after a night in the county funhouse. She was all dolled up, looking like a supermodel right off the runway. Her spoiled and prissy ways didn't seem to matter to me anymore.

After she smothered me with a barrage of kisses and a warm loving hug, she let go and slapped the shit out of me. Right across the face. Right in front of everybody.

"What do you mean going to jail like that? What did you do, Luis?" berating me past embarrassment. "And not calling me or anything!" Then she slapped the shit out of me again, "I was so worried." Topped off by another loving hug, "Oh, I was so worried. I love you so much, Louie."

My private thoughts were, "This woman is crazy...but at least she loves me, and I like the way she smells."

"Amelia, did you bail me out?" I asked her, "How'd you know I was in jail?"

She turned me loose and looked at me, "Cade and Theresa called me. They saw you on the TV news, Louie."

"What about my mother?"

"I don't think Anna knows yet."

Cade was at the desk signing my bail/bond papers. He was all of six feet, lanky, and under a cowboy hat. Bigger than life he stood there, my *gringo* friend coming to my rescue to get my sorry ass out of jail because I couldn't keep my mouth shut. I was just glad he had the money to do so.

When he walked up to me, we shook hands.

"You okay, Luis? You didn't become anybody's bitch in there did you?" Cade asked with a smile.

"That's not as funny as you think. Where's Theresa?" I asked.

"She's out in the truck waiting for all of us."

When we walked out into the parking lot, Theresa was standing there next to their Ford Dually. She was every bit of a tall Texas cowgirl, and she could back up the image. She could do everything on a ranch that any ranch hand could do. Out of the four of us, Theresa was probably the most level-headed too.

It felt good to get that hug from Theresa. "You okay, Luis?" she asked.

"I'm fine—until I get to my mother's. Then she'll probably slap me too."

Cade stepped up and solved that problem, "We made a plan, *amigo*. Me and Theresa thought it might be better if you and Amelia come to the house with us for the weekend."

I glanced at Amelia as she smiled and nodded her head. You could tell Amelia wanted to go. "Oh yeah?"

"Let things calm down a little. You know?" Cade explained.

"Sounds good to me. What about paying for my sins?" I asked him.

"You can help me with a pasture move, and we'll be even. How about that?" Cade explained.

"Yeah. I don't mind one bit. You ought to know that." I was trying to be gracious, but probed for the catch, "You had this planned all along. Didn't you? How much am I worth anyway?"

"A thousand dollars."

My jaw dropped in disbelief, "A thousand, that's all?" I was insulted. To the system, I was small potatoes.

As we all started to get in the truck, Amelia changed her mind about which side she was going to load and followed me.

"Sorry *compadre*." Cade explained, "They just ain't paying for Mexican outlaws like the old days. You'll have to try harder next time."

"I feel cheap," I whined. Then I noticed Amelia right on my heels. I couldn't walk normally. She kept stepping on my heels, "Amelia. What are you doing?"

Amelia gave me a reason that only made sense to her, "There's a grasshopper on that side, Louie. I thought he might jump on me."

Theresa was watching me roll my eyes and started to laugh. I was the last one to shut the door.

"I don't know about y'all, but this Mexican outlaw is hungry," I said with some force. "I haven't eaten anything since yesterday."

▼ ▼ ▼

Cade Ferguson was about four years older than me and four inches taller. He was one tall and lean *gringo*, and as most people that knew him would say, "He didn't take no shit from nobody."

The only way to get a good picture of what kind of man Cade was, you had to be told about his past. Like the time when he was a senior in high school and we were all attending a John Marshall High School football game in San Antonio. I was fourteen at the time, and Cade was sitting with me and my mother, Anna. Tony was playing in the football game, and the stands were packed.

It was a pretty normal game until someone from the stands threw a piece of trash over the crowd and hit Mrs. Reich in the back of the head. Mrs. Reich was one of our school's English teachers. Mrs. Reich's husband and everybody else turned around to see who threw the trash. It was thrown by the most notorious student and bad guy in the school, Ignacio Garza. He had been expelled from school several times, locked up in juvenile facilities, and well-known by the police ever since he was ten years old.

Mrs. Reich's husband didn't do anything about the incident even though he was a grown and capable man. He just sat there while Ignacio and his group of thugs laughed it up. But their laughter didn't last long.

Two cops that were attending the game walked halfway up the stands and motioned for Ignacio to come down to them. When Ignacio came into close proximity with Cade, they had words with each other, and they weren't cordial either.

Cade and Ignacio had been standing enemies at John Marshal High School ever since Ignacio figured out he couldn't push Cade around like the others in school. Over a four-year period, they accumulated a long history of altercations. Each time nearly coming to blows. Every time ended with Ignacio backing down to save the alignment of his own teeth, I'm sure.

This time it was different for Ignacio. He knew everyone was watching to see just how bad of an *hombre* he was. The cops' presence didn't deter Ignacio from giving Cade lip all the way down the stairs of the bleachers. That's when Cade decided to get up and follow him. Mom tried to stop him, but Cade's blood was rather hot at the time, and I don't think he heard a single word that Mom said.

The cops took Ignacio to a grassy open spot that was on the side of the bleachers. Most of us in the stands could still see what was happening.

The cops were giving Ignacio what they thought was "a good talking to," but somewhere during their scolding, they must have realized that nothing was sinking into his thick head. To make matters worse for Ignacio, he threatened to whip Cade's ass in front of the entire group.

When Cade walked closer, Ignacio put up his fist and pretended he wanted to fight. You had to give it to Ignacio, he put on a good show.

I don't know exactly what was said, but the cops took Cade and Ignacio farther back behind the stands and let them square off with each other, thinking they could settle their differences there and then. It was mutually agreed upon by both parties—like a police-sanctioned fight.

There was no time to take bets on who would win because Cade cleaned Ignacio's clock. Within fifteen seconds, Ignacio was down on the ground and motionless.

The cops immediately declared Cade the winner and sent him back to the stands. Then they performed the task of nursing Ignacio back to consciousness.

That was what I considered the "old days," when police around the country had more discretion in the field. They don't dare do that anymore.

As Cade walked back into the stands and started to sit down next to me and Mom, most of the crowd stood and applauded Cade. He was everyone's hero that day. I never realized until then, he was ten feet tall.

The final score that night: South San 17, John Marshall 20.

There are those that claim to be friends, but when times get hard, many of them cut and run. Everyone knows that no matter how right a man may be, there are times you've got to endure loss and suffer pain. That side of Cade's character was tested one night during a rodeo in Robstown, Texas.

A few years earlier during a rodeo in Robstown, Texas, Tony and I made the mistake of talking to one of the judges about our time in the team roping event. We felt he was cheating, but we didn't know exactly how.

Within seconds, the judge came off his hinges and was fighting me and Tony both. To make matters worse for us, a few of his friends saw it, quickly jumped the fences, and joined in against us.

Cade saw us being pummeled and swooped in like Tarzan to the rescue, trying to whip everyone's ass at once. We lost. All three of us got our asses whipped royalty. After the fight was over and they left us there in the livestock pens, we were slow to get up. Our bloody wounds were coagulating in horse and cow shit. How anyone never came down with tetanus or anthrax was a miracle.

You know what they say—you can't win them all. Maybe Cade knew it all along, but a man with that kind of honor won't stand by and do nothing. He's going to jump in the middle of the shit for his friends and family every time.

Cade lived on a giant ranch in the Texas Hill Country. In his adult life, he became well-known as an excavation contractor in the Bexar County area, carrying a lot of creditability around the Alamo city.

We had always been good friends. Everyone in Cade's immediate family had passed. The only other family he had was his wife, Theresa. It was the best move he ever made because she was the smartest one of all of us.

When Amelia married into the family, we would often stay on his ranch, where we always knew there would be lots of barbecue and drinks on hand. In turn, I would volunteer Tony and me for our services during his spring roundups. He always had a shortage of men that could ride a horse, so two De Zavala *vaqueros* were just the ticket for his needs.

More importantly, Cade was like the older brother to Tony and me. Sometimes we got along better with each other than we did with our own families.

To this very day I pray that I'll never be forced to appreciate my friends because of a loss. The De Zavalas didn't need a tragic loss to know that. We always considered them as family, and they us. There had always been Cade and Theresa, my *gringo* friends.

# 6.

# The Ferguson Ranch

The trade-off was always fair. I'd give him a day's work and he'd put us up in his adjoining guest cabin to the main house. Every time I went to Cade's, it was like taking a break from the demands and noise of the big city. Theresa was a great cook, so the food was always great and there was always plenty of cold beer after a work day. As for Amelia, she was excited every time we got a chance to go. To her, it was always like a paid vacation.

Cade used me to help rotate livestock about four times a year and once a year for a sale barn auction.

By topographical layout, there was a big difference between his ranch and other ranches in the area. He owned twelve thousand acres of the roughest, most treacherous hills in the Texas Hill Country and had a high perimeter fence around the whole damn thing. The only other fences on the ranch divided the ranch into four separate sections. Besides the pens, that was it.

The hills were covered with thick cedar, dangerous rock cliffs that would sicken a man's stomach to look over the edge, and deep dark gullies overgrown with thick brush that concealed every wild hog in the country.

You couldn't compare Cade and Theresa's ranch to other ranches in that part of the country. On most modern ranches you can round up livestock by honking the horn of your truck or go get them on a four-wheel ATV, but not on Cade's. The only way you could get around their ranch was on horseback. The old way.

We tried three-wheelers when they first came out, then four-wheeling ATVs, but they all had the tendency to roll over, injuring the driver. If you ran out of gas or had mechanical problems when you were on top of those hills, it was often impossible to get a truck there for a recovery. But the biggest problem was that the ATV didn't have a brain. That's when the twenty-first century yielded to the thinking process of a horse.

When a horse comes to thick brush, he will duck his head and walk right through the middle of the thickest part if he's trained. The same can be said when pushing a herd and a stray tries to wing off into the brush. A horse will see that before you do and react before a rider can touch the reins. They see things you can't, especially in the dark, and often keep you out of danger, whether you realize it or not.

Cade inherited the ranch from his father, who inherited it from his grandfather. He grew up knowing about ranch and construction work.

Tony and I learned all about horses, cattle, and goats from Papa Sergio. We spent our summers working with Papa Sergio when the other grandkids never dared to come around. That was our education away from home, since it gave Tony and me an invaluable skill set in the ways of the *vaquero*, and generated countless opportunities that others never received.

Papa Sergio was a great teacher, a skilled *vaquero* in his days and regarded by many as a *charro* of the highest order.

♥ ♥ ♥

Saturday morning Cade and I met in the kitchen where Theresa and Amelia were cooking breakfast. We both grabbed a cup of coffee and sat down at the table, then the girls started to bring in the food. This was a working ranch atmosphere with friends and soon-to-be family.

Amelia brought me a smaller-than-usual plate, piled with bacon, eggs, and biscuits and smothered in gravy that was dripping over the edges.

"Careful," I said. "There's too much on this plate."

"Theresa said to hold it over the fan a little while and let the grease congeal everything together," Amelia explained.

Cade asked Theresa, "Theresa, you giving chemistry lessons in there?"

Theresa walked up to Cade and put her arm around his shoulder, "Among other things."

"What other things?" I asked.

"How to be a rancher's wife, for one. She wants to learn," Theresa explained.

"That's great," nodding my head. "It really is—except we ain't got no ranch."

"Not to worry, Louie. I've got that all planned out. I'm going to sell instructional videos on the internet and make a million dollars for us. Then we can buy a ranch."

"What kind of videos?" I asked.

"My first video will be on dog training—how to turn your dog into a vegetarian," she told everyone.

Cade came alive, "Oh, I got to see that shit." Pointing out the window at the family dog, "Hell, Amelia! I'll donate a dog for you to train right now."

I love Amelia from the bottom of my heart. I really do, but the ideas she came up with sometimes worried me to the core. Sometimes I think my friends fed her schemes just to keep me constantly off balance.

❦ ❦ ❦

Cade and I pushed about four-hundred goats and about twenty cows that day. If you had patience and didn't crowd the herd, then two men could keep them pushed up against the fence line all the way to the open gates of the next pasture. It was an easy two-man job.

The highlight of that day was when we rode to the top of the mountains. We could see for miles, all the way to Highway 173. Cade's fence line went all the way up to the road.

Our little drive was going pretty smooth, so we pulled up our horses and took a good look around.

"Best view on the whole ranch," Cade said.

"A man could do some real thinking up here."

"Yeah," Cade agreed. "Too bad we couldn't live up here...leave all our problems. But you know...got to always go back down and face it."

I reined my horse back to trail the goats. "Face what? You got everything."

"Keeping fifty people employed is the biggest one," Cade voiced his concerns, "bidding and negotiating....keeping everyone satisfied while juggling a million details."

"That don't sound that bad," I told him blindly.

"Of course, my problems don't compare to yours, *compadre*."

"What problems are you referring to?" I asked.

Cade started grinning imitating Amelia's voice, "Louie! I got burrs in my panties. Come and help me, Louie! There's a bugger in my nose! What'll I do?"

"Okay, I get it. She's needy. It's something we're going to work on."

Who better than I would know that Cade was rattling my chain? That's the way we talked to each other, and it usually got worse when we started to drink.

After we closed the final gate on the herd, we trotted back to the ranch and tied up underneath the covered paddock. There was a refrigerator against the wall full of cold drinks and an anvil mounted on a stump next to a post. We had plenty of daylight left so we decided to jerk the shoes off of our horses and do a reset.

It was sure nice to down that first cold beer after pushing through the cedar in the heat all day. Papa Sergio often reminded me that in his days, there were no cold drinks. All they had was the coolness of water from creeks and springs.

Such were the stories of the old days, as told to us by the *vaqueros* and cowboys of the older generation. Their stories burned images into our minds. They left the smell of leather, the perfections of a good horse, and the measure of good men that understood ranch life ingrained in our minds to romance us.

"Well. Those shoes ain't going to pull themselves off," Cade said.

I sat down my beer, then walked over to my horse and lifted his hoof. My thoughts were still up on top of the mountain, "I didn't see many goat carcasses this time."

"It's them wild hogs," Cade explained. "They developed a taste for meat. I don't know how, but now they'll eat anything sick or dead. Bones, hair...it don't matter."

That was when Amelia walked up and started to pet the horse. "Cade, can I brush your horse?"

"Sure you can." Pointing to one of the tack rooms, "There's a curry comb and a brush in that tack room on the right."

It hit me two seconds after Cade told her where the curry comb was—it was not a good idea to go inside that first tack room on the right. So, before she got there, and with a noticeable concern in my voice, I blurted out, "No, wait, Amelia. Don't go in there."

Cade dropped his hoof and stood up, "Why not? That's where I put it."

I didn't have a plan, "The light's out in that room," I told her with a meek voice, "and it's dark in there...and there's spiders?"

Amelia cocked her hips and gave me a look like my mother always did, "Louie? What do you have in there, dirty magazines or something?"

"No," I whined.

"I'm not afraid of the dark, Louie. Besides, Theresa said if I wanted to become a rancher's wife, I should get tougher. I don't need any help. If I do, I'll call your name."

Cade stepped up next to me, watching Amelia walk into that dark tack room, and started to grin. Then he murmured to me, "You think she knows what a Daddy Long Legs is?"

"No."

Cade held up his cell phone, ready to record the action.

As she walked to the door, my smile disappeared, "This ain't going to be funny."

Amelia walked inside the dark tack room and felt around for the brush. It was true, the light was really burned out. This caused her to fumble around in the dark, unnecessarily bumping into saddles and making a lot of commotion.

This normally wouldn't be that big of a deal except for the thousands of Daddy Long Legs spiders that had conglomerated above her head in the darkest corner of the tack room. They're non-venomous spiders, and they have eight very long legs. Hence the name, Daddy Long Legs.

During the day, they find dark places to huddle together and stay there until something or someone disturbs them. When disturbed, they will pulsate like some critter's heartbeat in a monster movie.

As true as the setup was for all the things that were about to go wrong, all that bumping around caused a glob of spiders to drop from the ceiling, right on top of Amelia's head.

I figure the first glob of Daddy Long Legs that fell was in the number of five hundred spiders. That makes it about four thousand little spider legs crawling all over Amelia's perfections, and believe me, Amelia felt every one of those spider feet.

She came out of the tack room, trying to suppress her panic, but that didn't last long. Very quickly she began to flail her head in all directions, messing up her hair and then beating herself about the body.

Her full-time freak-out mode caused our horses to set back on their leads and knock over the anvil with the tools. Only at the end, when she couldn't hold her breath any longer, did she cry out for help.

Amelia got over the incident fairly quickly, but Theresa knew better and dumped our suppers in the garbage can. Then, you might say, the girls sequestrated themselves from us for the rest of the night. That was our punishment.

There was nothing left for us to do except go to the barn, play cards, and drink some more. We had everything we needed. There was plenty of beer in the fridge, and I found an old, opened bag of potato chips there for us to munch on.

I dealt the first hand, and we looked at our cards, "Is this what you call 'being in the dog house,' Cade?"

"Uh-huh."

"Well, I don't think I like it very much," I told him.

"Get used to it, *compadre*. Shit happens."

I put my cards down and looked into the darkness, "You know, I love Amelia, but I have yet to figure out what she's good at."

Cade laid down two cards and took two from the deck, "She ain't got to be good for anything. She's just got to be there and love you."

I laid down two and took two. "How many times in the future am I going to go to the dog house? That's what I'd like to know."

Cade started to grin, "Oh, an untrained husband like yourself, I'd say about a hundred."

I laid my cards on the table, "You know what? You're not helping my morale. So, I'm going to tell you what I'm going to do. Right from the start, I'm not going to allow the dog house to happen. No dog house in my house."

"How you going to do that?" Cade asked.

What came out of my mouth from that point on didn't make any sense. I wasn't used to drinking on an empty stomach. Neither was Cade.

"My rule as head of the household will be - she can never get mad and use the dog house against me."

Cade threw down his cards face up, "She don't need the dog house to torture you, Luis. Women got a million other ways. Take it from me, you'd be out of your mind to do that to a woman. Especially your wife."

"I think if I can solve the problem before it starts I'll be the smartest Meskin in the country."

Cade shuffled the cards, "Oh, yeah?"

"Yeah. Someday you'll see I was right. You can't be a *gringo* all your life, you know," then I reached into the bag of chips and pulled one out without looking.

Theresa and Amelia also walked up carrying two plates of food.

I guessed they finally forgave us.

As soon as I bit into the chip, I knew something was wrong. It tasted awful, so I spit it out. Within seconds I was hanging my head over the ground and a long string of drool was hanging from my mouth all the way to the ground. I couldn't seem to spit all of it out.

"Those chips taste like shit!" I complained.

"What's wrong with him?" Theresa asked.

"The smartest Meskin in the room just tried to eat one of my ear tags laced with malathion," Cade laughed and then told me, "I was saving them for the goats, you know?"

"Is he going to live?" Amelia asked.

"Yeah, he'll be okay," then he said to me, "Spit on the dog, Luis. He needs a flea collar anyway."

♦ ♦ ♦

Sunday morning, Tony drove up to the house in my almost brand new double cab Ford pickup truck. In the back of the truck were the luggage and gear for all of us. We were going on a rock-hunting trip with Tony.

Tony had always been a rock hound. He liked to collect pretty and unusual rocks more than he liked to dig for arrowheads. So, Amelia came up with the big idea to treat Tony to one last rock-hunting trip before he had to show up for the army. That was two weeks away.

Our plan was to travel all the way to the east side of New Mexico if we had to, stopping at every roadside rock shop and unusual tourist attraction we could find, and fill his pockets with rocks he considered to be collectible. The plan was that I would save the rocks until he got out of the service.

I was all in. Of course I was. Even though I was more into the archaeological world than rocks, I looked forward to this one last small adventure with my brother and my girl.

Tony missed out on all the work and fun, but he made it just in time for the big Sunday lunch that he knew Theresa and Amelia were fixing.

Cade met him at the door and brought him into the house. The living room had a huge ceiling. The rafters and exposed joists were made of giant timbers to make it look rustic in the western way. On the walls hung a variety of deer, wild boar, Aoudad sheep, elk, and other wild animal mounts he either shot or inherited over the years.

However, one of Cade's walls was covered in arrowhead and artifact collections. They were all encased in glassed picture frames, symmetrically aligned and positioned to be appealing to the eye. A fantastic collection of flint and chert spear points, ceremonial pieces, and surviving organics that didn't quite make it to the stage of total decay.

Tony had seen Cade's collection a hundred times before, but this time as he took off his jacket and decided to pay attention for some reason, "Your collection is what you see in museums, Cade. I guess you know that?"

"Yeah. That's why I got everything insured."

While they were talking, Amelia took a large book off one of the shelves, "*The History of Bandera County*?" she asked herself.

We all sat down and had a great meal. You might call it a traditional Sunday meal of fried chicken, mashed potatoes, enchiladas, fajitas, and lots of tortillas.

"How do you know they'll dismiss the charges?" I asked Cade.

"I don't know. It's just a guess. The thing is, Wilson's got too many irons in the fire for this kind of publicity...and if they went to court, he knows he'd be testifying about that ninth keg."

Tony exhaled loudly and shook his head, "The hell with that ninth keg. I'm tired of talking about it. You know how close I came to getting arrested?"

Then Theresa decided to wake us up, "Tony's got a point. This could have just as easily gone the other way. You'd still be in jail, Luis—and if Tony was arrested—the army ain't going to take him."

"Thank you, Theresa," Tony said to Theresa, then looked at us, "I got plans you know."

"You mean the plans of becoming a Green Beret?" I asked.

"I'm going into the combat engineers—and yes, after my hitch I'll have enough saved to go to college. That, along with the GI Bill, and I can go to school and get my degree in geology." He looked at everyone, frozen in place, "I want to become a geologist."

Theresa spoke first, "Good for you, Tony."

"I think that's a great idea," Amelia added.

"You never told me that," I said.

It was like Tony let out a long-held breath of air, "All this time, I could barely keep quiet about it," shaking his head with obvious relief from holding the secret. "One Indiana 'pinche' Zavala in the family is enough."

No one was extremely shocked by the news, but we were all mildly surprised. This wasn't like Tony to hold a secret and make such big plans. We were all silent but proud of him for making the choice and taking the steps.

"Well, one thing is for sure," Cade added, "you won't have Wilson looking over your shoulder anymore."

"That's for sure. Wilson reminds me of Zebu Taylor. I was always worried about Zebu coming around some corner, knocking me to the ground, and making me eat dirt."

"That's terrible," sympathized Amelia.

"What does dirt taste like?" I had to ask.

Eleven years later, you could tell, that character named Zebu was still on Tony's mind. When Tony was young, Zebu was Tony's number one problem. Of course, he was young in those days. Since then, Tony grew up and now he was telling us what he really thought.

"You know? I know I never told anyone before, but I use to dread running into that guy. Even if it was an accident. After my army training, maybe I should find him and kick his ass."

Amelia still had her head down, looking through the book and listening at the same time, "So where is old Zebu now?"

There was a pause in the conversation, then Cade spoke in a low tone, "He got his arm caught in a hay-baler. He lived—but, he had to learn how to use his left hand when he picks his nose."

Tony threw up his arms in defeat, "Well. That ain't the first time I ever shot myself in the foot...and for that, I'm sorry for Zebu."

Amelia slowly looked up from her book with a blank stare, but her reaction wasn't from what happened to Zebu. You could tell she was thinking about something else, calculating, and so it came to the surface in a question, "How long have you known each other? You remember when you first met?"

That was unexpected. It was such a simple question, and yet we couldn't come up with anything definitive. Instead, we looked at each other, hoping the other one had the answer.

"I don't think I know," Cade said.

I looked at Amelia, "As far as I can remember, we've always been around...since we were little kids?"

Amelia gestured the book to Theresa and asked, "Theresa. Can I borrow this book?"

"Sure you can. Just bring it back when you're finished."

I wasn't finished rubbing it in, so I looked at Tony, "Lessons to be learned, little brother."

He knew I was talking about Zebu. That was a mild insult, so he returned fire, "Oh yeah? I'd say that the first lesson was on you, big brother. To that I mean, quit picking fights with Professor Wilson. You'll live longer if you stay out of the calaboose."

So I leaned in and ground another lesson in his face, "I'm not the one that wants to kick ass on a one-armed crippled man!"

"Where were you when I said I took it back?"

"All that pent-up energy?" I said. "But really brother, on a man with one arm?"

Tony threw up his arms, "Can anyone help me here?"

Cade leaned in and looked serious, "I think I can help." Cade pointed in one direction, "Just down the road they have a ranch for crippled children. I'm sure we can find you someone you can whip ass on down there."

"What?" Tony yelped.

"That's a good idea, Cade," I agreed with a straight face.

Tony pointed at both of us and stood up from the table, trying to leave, "Both of you are crazy."

"You need to get it out of your system, son!" Cade told Tony as he walked into the living room.

# 7.

## Trans-Pecos Rock Hunt

It took us all day to get to Marathon, Texas. By the time we arrived, it was dark and the specific rock shop Tony wanted to visit was close, so we got a motel and called it a day.

According to Tony, West Texas is where rocks become interesting and collectible. The whole region is seismically active. Fault lines run and crisscross all over the area with an occasional earthquake to remind you where you are. It's a land of ancient volcanoes and lava flows. When this place was active, it pushed all the pretty rocks and minerals to the surface. There they sat until the first curious man came walking by and started picking them up. The rest is a matter of what men did with those rocks.

The Trans-Pecos region is littered with all different kinds of minerals. All rock hounds like to collect these varieties. However, the only mineral the region didn't have for large mining operations seemed to be gold. There were silver, mercury, uranium, and other minerals that I could remember. I didn't know my rocks as well as Tony, but I did enjoy looking and collecting different samples for him.

The rock stores in Marathon didn't have what Tony was looking for. Of course, when I would ask him what he was looking for he would always tell me he didn't know, or that when he found it, he would know. He wasn't looking for anything specific, but rather on the interesting side of nature.

We didn't spend but about two hours in Marathon before we loaded back up and headed to Marfa. Marfa was known for its rock shops. The only problem was that most of them were owned and run by someone from California or New York. That's what it seemed like anyway, and because of that, they all stocked their stores with the same tourist trinkets and in the same general layout.

Tony was fingering through one of the store's rock bins that were full of pretty black and shiny rocks and started shaking his head. You could tell he had run into a dead end.

He got my attention, "Hey *vato*. Let's get out of here. This place is got nothing but tourist crap."

"There's nothing here you like?"

"Nothing. Let's go down the road."

Of course Amelia ran up to us from down the aisle, all excited about a rock she had found on one of the shelves, "Louie! Look at this. Isn't this pretty?" She put it in place on her neck where a necklace would be, "I could make this into a necklace. It's so shiny. What do you think?"

Tony looked at me, "Like I said..."

♦   ♦   ♦

We stopped at one last rock shop on the outside of town. This place was a little different. It was owned by a Marfa native. With one exception to his life's history, all he ever did was collect rocks and sell them to the tourists, and his name was Concho.

Concho was an old hippie. He had to be seventy years old and dressed something in the combination - between a twenty-first century Comanche and Willie Nelson. He had long braided hair, a red beard, a few feathers here and there, and wore a leather vest that he obviously made himself. Concho was the coolest dude in town and everyone local knew him.

That one exception to his life's long history was hanging on the wall for everyone to see. As soon as customers walked in the front door, there was an old cut-out newspaper article hanging in the most strategic spot. With the article was a picture of what appeared to be Concho when he was a young long-haired hippie type, and he was embracing probably the ugliest dog I think I have ever seen. To make matters even more disturbing, it looked like the animal had no ears and only one eye, just like his caretaker. The caption on the newspaper read, "Marfa Man Nurses *chupacabra* Back to Health."

"You have got to be kidding me!" I said aloud and in disbelief.

"Believe it!" Concho shouted at me.

While Amelia started to look around the shop, I stood up straight and slowly walked over to the counter where Concho was, "Come on man! There ain't no such thing. If there was, we'd of had that thing in a cage by now."

Concho gave it a quick thought and then gave in, "Congratu-lations, whatever your name is! You just unraveled the mystery and popped my bubble," he mildly complained with disappointment in his voice. "But don't tell anybody. Tourists eat that shit up. The truth is, they're good for business...and I always need the business."

I stuck out my hand, "Luis De Zavala."

He returned the handshake, "They call me Concho."

"So what's that in the picture, Concho?" I asked, "There's got to be a good story behind it."

Since one of his eyes was covered with a patch, he tilted his head and focused on me with his good one, "Well, I can tell you, Luis, but you got to be careful who you tell. I don't want any trouble with the law, you know."

"Something was illegal?" I asked.

"Oh, I'm sure it was...it was in 1973," pretending to look around, as if anyone was listening. "I don't know what the statute of limitations is."

"1973?" I said, "Whatever it was I'm sure nobody cares anymore."

"That's good to hear," acting relieved.

What he told me next, I didn't know what to think. Concho could have been influenced by the occasional ghost voices that we can't hear, making him occasionally jerk his head sideways a tick, acting semi-dra-matic about everything.

"You see, when I was younger and dumber, I decided to become a drug smuggler. That's where the money was at, but I didn't want to mess with the border crossings cause that's where the trouble was. So I devised a way to get the drugs over the Rio Grande in an unconventional way - I would go to the Mexican side of the river and send the drugs over the river in a rocket machine. A rocket machine that I built myself."

"You built your own rocket?" I asked in amazement.

"That's right. The only problem I had was the type of propellant I used—a fifty-percent solution of hydrogen peroxide. I don't know if you know it or not, but that's some nasty shit."

"I know a little, but I've never messed with any."

"Take my advice and don't," Concho warned me. "It ain't like the stuff you find in the drug store. Anyway, I arranged a meeting with one of the Mexican honchos to give him a demonstration. It was just me, the head honcho, his two bodyguards, and a stray dog that followed us out in the brush. You see, the dog didn't belong to anybody. It was looking for a handout."

"You must have some big balls, Concho. Dealing with a drug lord in a foreign country and a rocket?" I said trying to compliment him.

"I did at one time," he continued, "but that hydrogen peroxide made them crawl up around my liver somewhere. You see, when I hit the go button on the rocket machine, something went terribly wrong and hydrogen peroxide exploded all over the place. We all took cover the best we could and everyone came out of the incident, I would say, lucky. But the stray dog wasn't so lucky. That stuff went all over his body. It must have hurt too, cause he hollered and yelped, and was smoking when he was running in circles. I could hear the little fucker squealing in pain as he ran through the brush and clean out of sight."

"My god, Concho," I said. "Did anything good come out of that?"

"Yeah!" Concho told me, "They didn't shoot me. That was a plus. Of course, I lost my potential rocket machine contract with the drug guys. There wasn't anything to do when I came back home to Marfa except sell rocks to the tourists. I wasn't making any money, but

I was hopeful for the future. Then one day out of the blue, that same dog walked up to me and we stared at each other, eye to eye. It was like he wanted revenge or K-9 compensation, or something."

I pointed at the picture and tried to understand, "You're telling me that dog crossed the river and found you in Marfa?"

"Yep," Concho continued, "and he was in a hell of a shape too. All his hair was gone...one eye was poked out...only little nubs for ears. He looked pitiful...but feeling responsible, I took him in and nursed him back to full health. He never grew any of his hair back and never looked like a dog again. But oddly enough, the tourists loved him. They didn't think he was a dog at all. So I started telling everybody he was a *chupacabra*. Hell, I got more business and attention over my *chupacabra* dog than I ever did selling rocks."

"You still got him?" I asked.

"Nope," Concho shook his head in remorse, "I lost my *chupacabra* dog years ago. Sure do miss him too. He was more popular than I ever was."

"That is one hell of a story," trying to compliment him. "If I never picked up another rock again, that story would have been worth the trip."

"So who's the rock hound in your group?" Concho asked.
I motioned towards my brother, "My brother, Tony. Here he comes."

Tony walked up to Concho's counter with a handful of rocks and laid them down. I walked over to join Amelia.

Concho looked at Tony and complimented him on his choices, "I see you got all the basics...all the important stuff. You do a lot of collecting?"

"Not as much as I'd like," Tony told him. "This will be my last hunt for a while. I got to do a hitch in the service in about two weeks."

Me myself? I wasn't about to find anything as interesting as the story of the hairless *chupacabra* dog, so I walked over to where Amelia was, and when I thought no one was looking, I grabbed her by the ass cheek. It fit in my right hand perfectly. She hit me in the head with a piece of calcite. (That's a rock with sharp edges.)

Someone once told me that when a girl throws rocks at you, it means she likes you. I guess the more stars I saw, the more love set itself deep within.

When Amelia and I finally reached the counter with a few rocks of our own, Tony and Concho were in a deep conversation.

"Luis," filling me in, "Mr. Concho is telling me about a place we need to go."

"Where's that?" I asked.

Concho spoke up and filled me and Amelia in, "Sierra Blanca. There's an old Mexican couple there that had a rock shop in the old days."

"You're saying he had a rock shop?" I asked.

Concho filled us in, "It's like this. About ten years ago, Trini and Martha Lopez—those were their names—had a rock shop there in the downtown area. They had been there for, I don't know, forty years? About ten years ago, his wife Martha died, so Trini closed the shop and moved everything to his house. He officially retired. But really, I think he just missed his wife and gave up."

Amelia frowned, grabbed me by the arm, and held on tight, "That's such a sad story."

"So, what happened?" Tony pressed on for the rest of the story, "Tell us more."

"Trini had people continue to bring him some fantastic collectibles for the next ten years," Concho explained, "and all Trini did was let it stockpile in his backyard. Those rocks have been laying there for the last ten years, doing nothing. Nobody's looked through it that I know of."

"Will he talk to us?" Tony asked.

"Yeah, I think so," Concho told us with calculated confidence. "Yeah, I think so, but you can't call him. He doesn't have a phone."

I added, "I mean, we got money. We can pay."

"That's good," Concho said, "because the last time I heard, Trini wasn't doing so good. He could probably use the money, I'm sure. And man," looking at Tony, "you would have a good chance of getting some rare finds. There's no telling what's in that pile of his."

"I'm going to write down his address." Concho scribbled the address on an old receipt and gave it to Tony, "Here. Ever since his wife died, he kind of withdrew into himself. He doesn't see many people anymore. He's got no family, and lately I heard that he's been hearing things or something. I don't know."

Tony put his hand out to shake, "Concho, I want to thank you. When we leave there, I promise you he'll have more than he did before."

"I'll bet he could use some groceries too?" I asked Concho.

"Probably so."

I tried to convey to Concho that all would be good when we got there. "We'll take care of it. We got a grandfather too, you know."

"What's his name?" Concho asked as we opened the door.

"Sergio De Zavala," I proudly told him as I shut the door.

"Old Sergio would be proud, I think," Concho muttered to himself.

Before we got to Sierra Blanca, Trini Lopez became a figure of speculative mystery. We talked about him the whole way there. As young adults we were seldom offered the opportunity to be significant in our daily lives. Now that we had that chance, we felt like we had a purpose.

The drive from Marfa, through Alpine and on to Ft. Stockton, is one of the most scenic routes a Texan can take. It's full of mountains on both sides of the road. The clear crisp air, blue skies, windy roads, and fantastic rock formations that were along the road were not something we were used to seeing. It was all beautiful, and hours of driving passed by like minutes.

We weren't going to make it to Sierra Blanca before dark because we left too late; however, we knew that before we left. So we planned on stopping and spending the night in Van Horn. Amelia had a chance to buy some groceries for Trini Lopez, while Tony and I set up camp for the night at an RV park.

Everything Amelia bought was non-perishable. She bought two paper bags full of groceries—everything that older people eat or need from time to time. She was a wizard in the department of what people needed or wanted.

❦ ❦ ❦

That night we all lay down at the picnic table and looked at the stars. They seemed clearer out there than in the Hill Country. Desert air? Cleaner air? I didn't know.

"The sky sure is beautiful," Amelia said.

"I don't think I've seen this many stars before," I added.

We heard Tony take a deep breath, "I guess that wherever they send me, I'll be able to see the same stars—wherever I go."

A good thirty seconds passed before I said something. I had to think. "You better come back to us, brother. In one piece."

Amelia reached over and grabbed me by the hand. Whenever I thought we were as close as two people could be, she continuously amazed me, over and over at the love she was able to give me.

# 8.

# Trini Lopez

Sierra Blanca survives on less than four inches of rainfall per year. Honestly, I don't know how they do it. To me, it's just too damn dry for someone that is accustomed to rain throughout the year. On one side of town, dead trees were everywhere. It looked like the residents had pulled up stakes and abandoned the entire town. What trees were still alive were so gnarly-looking they looked like they belonged in the front yard of the *Adams Family* movie set.

Years ago, mining, ranching, and oil were king in Sierra Blanca. That was the place to be, but those days were long gone. Only a fraction of the people lived there now.

According to my electronic street finder, Trini Lopez's house was outside the city. We followed the route until we were there and didn't even realize it until we were right on top of it. There stood an old house that needed more attention than a simple paint job. Somebody needed to close the windows and shut the doors. Everything was wide open for the dust and wind to blow in one side of the house and out the other. There was a picket fence around the house but no dog to keep in, and the corners of his fence lines were piled with dried and stiffened tumbleweeds. It looked abandoned.

We arrived at Trini Lopez's house at about that time of day when the wind starts to pick up and blow hard. That's a daily occurrence for summertime in that part of west Texas and locals know it gets worse as the day goes by. It was our intention that we get our business done before the winds and the dust were too much.

From the street, we could see an assortment of small barns and sheds. Along the walls on the outside of the barns and sheds were two very long tables. Even from the street, we could see that those tables were holding Trini's rock collections. There were so many rocks piled on the tables that the tables were sagging from the weight.

All three of us walked up to the front door and expected to knock and introduce ourselves, but it didn't happen that way. The screen door was busted and you could see straight through the house and through the back door.

"Anybody here?" Tony yelled.

We waited for a moment, then it became obvious. Nobody was home.

I urged everyone to forget the front door approach, "Nobody's home. Let's walk around back."

We walked around the house to the backyard and found him in the only spot of shade from the only tree in the yard. He was sitting quietly in his lawn chair, wearing an old cowboy hat and staring into the western sky. That was Trini Lopez.

He was pushing the envelope into his late nineties and reached a point that so many elderly did where he became emaciated. Most commonly the result of refusing or forgetting to eat.

At that moment in time, we didn't give credit to the old man we saw in that lawn chair. After all, we knew nothing about him, only that time had probably locked away all his intimate secrets of life... or so we thought.

Trini Lopez didn't seem to notice us behind him, or maybe he just didn't care. We didn't know. I'm sure he had problems with his hearing as well as his eyesight at his age. It was obvious he was worn out by life and it left him in a feeble condition. He was "the old man" that had outlived his family and friends - abandoned in a world that he had nothing in common with nor could he understand. So he survived by existing in a world of hard times and a harsh climate.

Tony stepped in front of Trini and spoke to him, "Mr. Lopez? My name is Tony De Zavala. This is my brother..."

Trini Lopez never moved. His only acknowledgment of us was a glance of the eyes, but his head never turned.

I was watching closely. Tony was wasting his time. I had to interrupt, "Tony, I don't think he hears a thing you're saying."

Then for a new tactic. I bent over, looked him in the face and spoke louder. *"¿Señor López? ¿Está bien? Concho nos envió. Le trajimos comida y nos gustaría comprar algunas de sus rocas."*

I told him that his friend Concho sent us to buy some of his rock collection and that we brought him some groceries, but still I didn't seem to be reaching his conscious mind.

Trini's eyes kind of darted around all over the place. We couldn't tell where he was looking or if he even heard us. What was evident was that Trini responded more to Spanish. So, from that point on, we spoke to him in Spanish.

Amelia squatted down in front of him, placed her hand on his knee, and tried to ask if she could take his groceries to the house, *"¿Trino? Tengo dos bolsas de comida para ti. ¿Las puedo poner en la casa?"*

That's all it took. Trini's eyes lit up at the sound of Amelia's voice and he immediately came around, focusing on Amelia's face. It was as if he recognized her from somewhere in time.

The old man looked so emaciated from not eating right, I couldn't help but wonder who, if anyone, was taking care of him.

In as many physical problems that may have plagued him while sitting on the edge of life, he still managed to smile at Amelia. For that moment, I was relieved.

*"¿A dónde te fuiste? El caballo jaló la soga de mis manos."* Trini asked Amelia where she'd gone and rambled on about a horse that had pulled the rope from his hands. The story didn't make any sense to us, but Amelia stayed with him.

Tony asked Trini again, "Mr. Lopez. Will you sell us some of your rocks?"

Trini slowly looked up at Tony and nodded his head, *"Sí. Tómenlas."*

That was all the business Trini could tolerate for the day. After saying those few words to Tony, he went immediately back into his smile and looked at Amelia. Then he gently reached out to hold Amelia's hand that was still on his knee.

It seemed that for some reason Amelia felt compelled to gravitate to Trini. Although she had never met him before, she decided to go on an adventure of the imagination and be gracious enough to play the part of whoever Trini thought she was.

*"Tengo tanto que decirte. ¿Has visto a Martha?"*

Amelia looked up at me and said softly, "You guys go ahead. I think I'll stay here for a while."

Tony and I took about an hour to look through the entire rock collection. Every time we found something we liked, we put it to the side and started a pile of money on the table to be left with Trini.

*"Muchos, muchos días. No me gusta ese caballo. Dime, ¿has visto a Martha?"* Trini told her he didn't like the horse. And again, he asked if she'd seen Martha.

Amelia found herself going deeper and deeper down that rabbit hole Trini had dug. She may have not understood what he was talking about, but she became determined to find out and play along. Her compassion and her curiosity were her strengths.

She told him that she hadn't seen the horse and then asked him if he wanted anything to drink, *"Lo siento, Trino. No he visto ningún caballo. ¿Quieres algo de beber?"*

Trini pulled slightly on her arm, *"Quiero levantarme. Ayúdame."*

With some careful effort, Amelia stood Trini up and let him hold on to her arm for balance, *"¿A dónde vamos?"*

Trini pointed his bony finger to the far end of his property, *"A donde ella yace. A donde yo yaceré."* He told Amelia, "Where she lays. Where I will lay."

*"¿Martha?"* asked Amelia.

*"Sí,"* Trini answered.

Suddenly, Amelia had the good idea to ask Trini who he thought she was in a question, *"Trini, ¿cómo me llamo?*

*"Tú eres mi Lupe."*

Now that Trini called her Lupe, she knew who she was to him and could accommodate his vision.

It took them a few minutes to shuffle to the back side of the property. At one point Trini stopped and began to stare into a pile of brush. At first Amelia didn't notice anything, then she looked closer and saw something that was covered by the tumbleweeds.

Amelia turned loose of his arm and began to move the tumbleweeds. In that pile she found two unkept headstones. One had the name Martha Lopez, his deceased wife, and the other Lupe Lopez, Trini's deceased daughter.

While she was cleaning the tumbleweeds from the grave sites, Trini muttered the story. It was Lupe, his daughter, that was killed in a horse-riding accident in 1974. She was in the prime of her life at just eighteen years old.

Now everything made sense and Amelia suddenly realized how she fit into his thoughts.

Say what you want about the old man, but I never believed Trini was mentally ill. He simply had his facts and his time frames a little mixed up. That's all.

That time was a rough emotional moment for Amelia to overcome. The effects would linger with her, as would also with us, for a long time afterward. But before you start to feel sorry for her, remember this. There was no one else to hold his hand while he painfully recalled that time. Amelia was special because she chose to do so, knowing that Trini's realm had a short existence of time left. She considered it a privilege to do so.

When she walked back to Trini, he was wiping the tears from his eyes with a handkerchief he was carrying.

He told the story of how he was blessed with two loves, only to have God take them away. First his joy and then his love.

*"La gente más preciada con la que fui bendecido. Dios se llevó mi alegría. Y luego se llevó mi amor,"* Trini muttered in a low tone.

Amelia was doing her best to fight back the tears, but they still made their way to the surface, so she told him what he probably wanted to hear, *"Creo que Martha te está esperando,"* that Martha was probably waiting.

*"Ya quiero ir a verla. Ya no tengo nada aquí,"* he told her in a testy voice, saying he wanted to see her because he had nothing left.

She gently took his arm and held it like a daughter would, telling him she was there for him, *"Aquí estoy. Aquí estoy contigo."*

Before we loaded up all of the rocks we bought, a healthcare nurse dropped by. Trini was on her list of visits. It's a good thing too because even though we didn't know him, leaving him exactly where we found him, in the middle of the yard, was going to give us worry about him.

Before we left, I stuck a giant wad of money in his pocket and told the nurse about the groceries we put in the house. The last act out the door was when Amelia kissed Trini on the cheek and whispered something in his ear.

As we drove back towards Van Horn, Tony and I noticed that Amelia was not her usual bubbly self. A few miles down the road and she laid her head on my shoulder.

Tony and I believed that Amelia slew the demons of despair and loneliness that haunted Trini. Like an angel of mercy, she swooped down from the heavens, gave comfort to the needy, and left on a whirlwind of victory.

When I watched her cry into my shoulder trying to keep her feelings as private as she could, I realized that at that moment I had a whole new admiration for her and what she had done. An unknown talent no one knew she had. I seriously doubt that I could have ever summoned the fortitude to do the same thing she did for Trini Lopez.

♥ ♥ ♥

The next morning, we woke up in the same Van Horn RV Park that we were in the night before. The air was cool, the skies were clear blue, and we were all hungry for breakfast.

That last stop had put us over the edge of collecting rocks. Tony said we got more than he bargained for. It was time to go back home. But first we wanted to lay out some of our best rocks on the tailgate and give them a closer look.

"Man. That Concho was right," Tony said. "Trini had the mother lode of all collections.."

We placed them in a row all along the tailgate according to size and shape.

Then I picked up a giant piece of black granite and put it down. It must have weighed two pounds. "I had to get this," I told Tony. "It's got to be the biggest piece of shiny black granite I've ever seen."

"Looks like the piece I found," Tony said. Immediately he rummaged through his pile of rocks and pulled out another piece of black granite. It was about the same size as mine, so he put it down next to my piece and his eyes widened, "I'll be damned."

While we were admiring the similarities, Amelia innocently pushed the pieces next to each other. She turned them around and then over like a Rubik's cube, then pushed them together until they fit together perfectly. Those pieces belonged to each other. It was obvious. Somewhere along the way in its existence, it broke in half.

We all knew what the granite stone was in the shape of. This was no accident—it was as plain as the nose on our faces—but no one said a word. Tony and I just stared at it in disbelief. Our mouths were hanging open like two cavemen that suddenly discovered fire.

"Ho-lee-shit!" Tony blurted.

"I don't believe it," I added.

With her happy cheerleader voice and cuteness, Amelia looked at it and smiled. "It's a human heart!" she squeaked out. She turned around to give us a cute glance, then back to the black granite stone, *Es un corazón humano!*

# 9.

## The Rediscovery of the Black Heart Stone

She was right. Those two pieces of black granite that fit so perfectly together were in the shape of a human heart, and it wasn't by chance. Every intricate detail of it was accurate, like it was made as a study piece for medical students.

Tony rolled it over and looked at it on all sides, "This is not something you run into every day, or ever."

"It's going to be the best rock you ended up with on this trip," I told him.

"Oh no! This is archaeological, not geological..." Tony turned over the stone and ran his fingers over the heart, "You see this? The only thing I've ever seen made out of granite was tabletops. How someone made all of these polished this stone in such intricate detail to look like a human heart is beyond me. Everybody knows that if you start hammering and hacking on a piece of granite like this, it's most likely to break when you start to work with it. But you can see, it was once one single piece. For how long, no one can say."

Amelia asked, "Are you sure it's granite?"

"Pretty sure," Tony confirmed, "black granite. What's more, it's been shaped and polished." Then Tony looked at me, "What do you think, Mr. Archaeologist?"

I was stumped, so I came right out and said, "I don't have any idea, brother. I've never seen or heard of anything like this before... maybe from Central America? What time period? I have no idea. I'll have to make some phone calls."

We may have marveled at this black granite rock that was shaped like the human heart, but the mystery took the back seat to our growling stomachs. We packed up our gear, drove into Van Horn, and went to a restaurant for breakfast.

♥ ♥ ♥

Everyone seemed to forget about the black granite pieces we found until we got something to eat. Then we slowly got back to business.

I pushed my plate to the side, pulled out my phone, and started texting people.

"Who you calling?" Amelia asked.

I put my head to the phone, "I am going to send a picture of this rock to everyone in the Texas Artifact Diggers group. Maybe someone will know something."

"That's a good idea," Tony agreed, "but they're not archaeologists like you. No academic training, Luis. How would they know what they were even looking at?"

"They may not," I sat the phone down, "but as a collective... somebody might know something."

"You think that will do the trick?" Tony asked.

"I know one thing. When you put all the diggers together in one room, you increase your chances. To some of those guys it's more than a hobby...and if you'll recall, half of them have lived in other countries. That gives you different perspectives to a variety of problems."

"It's called networking," Amelia said. "You're networking, Louie."

I looked at her and smiled, "Yeah, increasing my chances...networking."

♥ ♥ ♥

There was one more place we wanted to go before we headed back to San Antonio and that was the Guadalupe Mountains. It was only about sixty miles north of Van Horn, and everyone wanted to see the highest point in the state of Texas, standing at over 8,700 feet in elevation.

Of course, that wasn't the only reason we were going. Tony was chasing an old treasure-hunting story about a man named Ben Sublett and a gold mine the old man drew ore from whenever he got low on funds. Sublett died in San Angelo in the early 1900s without revealing where the mine was. All anyone knew was that it was somewhere in the Guadalupe Mountains. Before he died, he told his son that the location didn't matter. All the gold was practically gone by that time anyway. The mine was never re-discovered.

You would think that would be enough deterrent not to look for the mine again. Again, legend had it that the mine didn't have any gold left. Tony wanted to say he chased the legend of the Sublett gold mine just to put a feather in his hat. Only the bragging rights. At the end of the day, I guess we could all say that.

The Guadalupe Mountains are absolutely beautiful. It was worth the drive, even if we never picked up another rock again for the whole trip.

Of course, we had to get out below the peak of El Capitan and pretend to look for the gold mine that was or wasn't there. It's a good thing we didn't find anything either since we were in a national park and they tend to frown on people that take things from the park. Even a lone rock.

At the end of the long day, we headed back to Van Horn for another final night. This time in a motel. Everyone agreed that we couldn't ride another day in the truck with each other and endure the smells that were fermenting. It was time to clean up.

West Texas is a very unique place. During the summer, the days start off cool with no wind. As the day progresses, it gets hotter and the winds pick up, generating a continuous stream of dust storms and wandering dust devils.

From an elevated vantage point, like a high mountain top, you can watch them below in the desert valleys, seemingly running a course from west to east, swirling and blowing, causing minor chaos for anything in their paths. And the nights are always beautiful.

After Amelia and I cleaned up, Tony knocked on our motel door and I answered it.

"Y'all ready to eat?" Tony asked.

"Yeah," I told him, "let me get my phone."

When I picked it up, I glanced to see how many people had called or left a message. I had it on silence earlier and had forgotten to turn it back on. There were about ten missed calls and twelve unseen text messages, all from our mother, Anna, and Cade Ferguson.

"Whoa!" Surprised as I was, "We got a load of messages here... all from Mom and Cade."

"That's it," Amelia said. "Your mom finally found out you got arrested and spent the night in jail."

Tony knew he was in the clear of any blame from Mom. "Yeah," he relaxed and said with confidence, "she's going to stab you in the ass with one of your own arrowheads."

We slowly wandered out into the parking lot and got in the truck. Nobody was in a hurry.

She wouldn't hurt me," trying to minimize the alarm, "I'm her firstborn."

♥ ♥ ♥

We took one of those booths in the corner of the restaurant. The kind that was shaped half round, had high back seats, and gave us some privacy. There weren't that many people in there anyway. We were fairly alone.

After the waitress gave us our menus, I took out my phone and started going through the messages and voicemails.

"Holy hell," I alerted everyone. "Every one of these messages sounds urgent. 'Call home, this is important' is repeated over and over. Even Cade."

"They didn't say about what?" Tony asked.

"No. I better call Cade first, get it straight from the horse's mouth." I dialed his number and put the phone up to my ear, "I hope everyone's okay."

Amelia made the sign of the cross, "Me too."

Cade answered the phone, and he was all business. "Hey man! Why haven't you been answering the phone?"

"I been up in the mountains. There's no signal up there you know. What's going on?" I asked with some concern.

"You know that picture you took and thought it would be a good idea to put in on the archaeological site? The black rock that looks like a heart?"

"Yeah. We still got it."

"Well, it's called the Black Heart Stone, and the last time it was seen was in 1935. Now, ask me how I found that out."

"How?"

"From your old buddy, Professor Wilson. He saw the picture on the web and called my house twice looking and asking about you. Hell, he even went to your house and talked to your mother."

"Oh shit. Is she mad at me?" I muttered.

"She's fine, Luis. We'll take care of Anna."

"I need to put you on speaker, Cade. Amelia and Tony need to hear this too."

Both of them leaned in over the table.

"All of you need to worry about Wilson," Cade warned us, "Everybody in the diggers group thinks that he's on his way to find you and seize that stone. Maybe put you in jail again. Nobody knows for certain."

"He can't do that Cade," Tony interjected. "We bought that stone legitimately—from a legitimate seller."

"Look. I have no doubt that you did," Cade assured us, "but the consensus says he wants to get his hands on it at any cost—before you can announce the discovery and alert the press."

We all blurted out insults to Wilson and the scheme he was most probably orchestrating. For just a moment, we lost our composure as a family group, talking over each other in loud and irritated tones. It wasn't a very becoming trait.

"Hold on!" I spoke up. "Everybody chill."

After we composed ourselves, I asked the golden question.

"Okay, Cade. What in the hell is so special about this stone?"

"I don't know, but it must be big. Wilson wouldn't say," Cade admitted, "but there's a man in Gatesville, Texas, that might. He's the grandson of the last recorded owner, Frank Simmons. That much I did find out. John Blake is the man you need to talk to. Simmons was his grandfather."

It was difficult to enjoy the rest of our breakfast. That phone call caused a thousand scenarios to run through my mind, most ending with my hands around the neck of Professor Wilson.

I knew this wasn't my fault, but I still felt guilty for getting Tony and Amelia in the middle of that mess. After all, Wilson was my nemesis, not theirs. I had to keep my composure. I was the oldest, as well as a husband-to-be.

Since we were ahead on our rock-hunting adventure and Wilson was after us, we decided to take a trip to Coryell County and find John Blake, grandson of the old treasure hunter and late author, Frank Simmons.

We looked at each other and all came to the same conclusion, we go straight to Gatesville on the back roads, track down this man named John Blake, and find out what was so special about the Black Heart Stone.

All we had to do was traverse the state from Van Horn to Gatesville and keep an eye out for vehicles marked *Texas Department of Natural Resources.* That was the markings of the Wilson gang, and we didn't want to rumble.

# 10.

## John Blake and the Long Story

We left Van Horn early the next morning, driving mostly the two-lane roads all the way to Gatesville. It took all day to drive the five-hundred miles, and most of the time we didn't see anything worth talking about. Truth be told, the whole trip we were on the lookout for Wilson and his two new and still "wet behind the ears" cops that were assigned to his department.

Nobody knew much about Professor Wilson except that he cracked a pretty hard whip when it came to antiquities and the law. Since he became the Director of Antiquities for the state, he managed to squeeze two law enforcement officers out of his budget. Unfortunately for our morale, we also learned that they were armed with real guns and real bullets.

Whether they had any experience or knowledge about artifacts and antiquities was as much of a mystery as if they were even needed. It could've been to curtail the artifacts trade. The raiding of archaeological sites was becoming big business for the black marketeers. I wasn't one of them, but Wilson never asked me what side I was on. He just harassed me like I was.

Tony and Amelia never met Wilson, so they had no idea what he looked like, nor could they put a prejudicial image on the man. I was the only one that had any dealings with him.

While we were on the road, Amelia asked me the same question again, but I was always changing my description.

"What does he look like?" she asked.

"He's got the face of a weasel and habits of a pack rat," I told her with disdain.

"That's not what you said two days ago," she told me.

"That's right," Tony said backing her up. "Last week you said he looked like a javelina and had the morals of a buzzard."

"That too."

That long stretch of road was a hot and tedious drive. Everyone was tired of sitting in one position for so long. My butt was itchy and numb, Tony had gas, and Amelia had to pee every fifty miles. We were looking for an excuse to stop.

About thirty miles before we got to Gatesville, we stopped and got another motel for the night. It was too late to start searching for John Blake. Besides, it was going to take some old-fashioned research to find him, and a fresh morning start was what we needed.

Tony and I finally called Mom. It was something both of us were dreading.

Like two bad sons, we postponed our phone call until we lost the signal out of Van Horn. When we would periodically get a signal, we avoided the call because of roaming charges. Then we'd lose the signal again and so on. We became masters of procrastination. Finally, Amelia made us face the music and make the call.

Mom could be a lot scarier than Wilson could be. When we were kids, she would get mad and threaten to "yank a knot in our ass" if we misbehaved. Luckily for us, we were too far away for her to yank anything out of us.

❦ ❦ ❦

We wasted no time the next morning. As soon as the sun was up, we were gone and entering Gatesville, looking for a library or the chamber of commerce, whichever we found first. We found the county library.

The head librarian was a very sweet elderly lady with thick glasses and a high-pitched, squeaky voice. It was a heavy Central Texas accent to be exact. She informed us without missing a beat that everyone in those parts knew about Frank Simmons. She added that although he had been dead for over seventy years, he was still well-revered as a local historian. His articles and books were so thorough that over time they used his grandson like a verifying reference book when it came to the history of Coryell and Bell counties. Everything was chronicled and stored at John Blake's house in remarkable detail.

"Simmons died before I was born," the librarian informed us, "but he was a treasure hunter from the old school of prospectors. Later on, he became a writer of books and magazine articles. If you can get inside Blake's house, you'll see that he's got his own library. It's huge. We don't have that many of Simmons' writings here."

Something she said caught my attention, so I leaned in and asked her, "What exactly did you mean by, 'if we can get inside the house?'"

"Didn't anyone tell you?" the librarian asked like she was surprised at our question. "John Blake is a rough old cobb...meanest person I ever did know."

"How old is he?" Tony asked.

The librarian cocked her head and thought about it, "I would put him at about his mid-eighties. Still, he's the meanest person I ever did see. Cantankerous without a reason...that's what I call him."

Tony squinched up his face in disbelief, "Oh come on! Nobody can be that mean!"

"You wanna bet?" countered the librarian in full rebuttal. "I seen him look a squirrel real hard and the poor squirrel just fell over dead... for no other reason than pure meanness."

Tony looked at me, "Beats using a shotgun, I guess."

"That's pretty mean," I tried to appease her, "but we can probably handle him."

"If he starts giving you the eye," she warned us, "don't stand there and trade stares. You best run away."

That was one description we would never forget. Now we couldn't wait to meet John Blake. The search suddenly became as much a curiosity as it was a search for information about the Black Heart Stone.

▼  ▼  ▼

John Blake lived in a giant old two-story house that was separated into two sections and probably built in the early 1900s. It had high ceilings and four built-in fireplaces in different parts of the house. What's more, it had a covered wooden porch that went completely around the house and a dog run in the middle. The style was a cross between plantation and early pioneer. In the early days, one could see that this was where civilization ended and the west began.

All three of us walked up onto the porch and to the screen door. I knocked twice, but nothing. So I knocked again, and nothing. So I knocked again.

"Hold your damn horses!" A voice echoed from inside the house, "A man can't even take a piss..."

The door opened and there stood John Blake. He may have been old, but you could tell he was a scrapper in his younger days. We stood there for a second and looked at each other through the screen door.

"What the hell! You from that church group, trying to get more donations?" Blake asked in a rough voice.

"No," Tony answered.

"Good," he opened the screen door, "then one of you must be Andrew Wilson."

Our mouths dropped.

"Oh no!" I blurted out. "Is he on his way...coming here?"

"If you ain't him, then yes. I talked to him about an hour ago," Blake said. "He called from San Angelo I believe."

Tony looked at me, "That means we've got a three-hour lead. No time to waste."

"If you ain't Wilson, then who the hell are you?" Blake demanded.

Pointing to each one of us, I introduced us, "Tony De Zavala, Amelia soon-to-be De Zavala, and I am Luis De Zavala. I think we have the Black Heart Stone."

John Blake's eyes opened wide, "You're the ones that have it?"

"Yes, we do," I told him, "and we need you to tell us the story behind it. Can you do that?"

"Of course, I can," replied Blake. "Come inside."

We all went inside his house, through the living room, and into the study, which was the library we had heard about. That entire inside of the house was like a museum. Blake never threw anything away. That was obvious by the looks of the place. There were hundreds of books on the shelves and pictures that covered every available inch of his walls.

Everyone kind of wandered around his library, independent of each other and in awe at his collection.

"How did y'all find out about me?" Blake asked as he plopped down in his favorite chair.

"We asked the librarian in town? Thick horned-rimmed glasses? High squeaky voice?"

"I know who you're talking about," Blake waived me off. "She's got a fine ass, but she blames me for the death of a damn squirrel...of all things!"

"She said you stared at it until it fell over dead?" Tony said in a questioning manner.

"Ah, bullshit!" Blake spurted out. "That squirrel was run over by a dump truck, and she knows it. She's just mad 'cause I took the squirrel home and threw it on the barbecue pit."

And here came Amelia, her mouth wide open, "You ate the poor squirrel?"

Blake put his hand over his brow and started to talk in a low controlled tone, but he was a little louder at the end, "Look. If you're going to take the side of that crazy old librarian, about a squirrel that should have died from old age fifty years ago, then I seriously doubt I can tell you about the Black Heart Stone before your good buddy Wilson gets here to kick your ass. You *sabe*?"

"Me *sabe*." I told him in total agreement.

"Now. One of you needs to get up and go get that stone. I want to take a picture of it and compare it to some drawings my grandfather sketched."

"I'll get it," Amelia volunteered and then walked out the door.

Then Blake leaned back in his big chair and looked me square in the eyes, "Before I tell you about the stone, you tell me your story, and why in the hell are you running from a state official?"

John Blake was all business. He might have been old, but I knew people like him. The most common mistake people could make with people like him was to underestimate his wit. He was a natural strategist, able to juggle a hundred details at once. He knew exactly what he was doing, and you couldn't fool a man like that. If you did, he would be able to see right through your bullshit.

Luckily, I had no lies. So, I told him the whole story, from the Lost Spanish Cache on the Salado Creek to buying the stone and arriving at his house.

Blake didn't say much. He sat there and listened. He acted like he was truly interested in what I had to say. However, the librarian was right about one thing, he was naturally mean. Before we got out of there, he managed to insult every one of us at least once.

Amelia brought the Black Heart Stone into the house, and Blake gently put the two pieces on a table with the broken sides towards each other.

"Yes indeed, this is it. The lost Black Heart Stone...since 1935," he told us and then took a picture.

"And?" I urged him.

"Yeah, Mr. Blake. What's the big deal about this thing?" Tony asked.

Blake took off his glasses and leaned back. That was obviously an annoying question. "The big deal is, this stone originated from an ancient culture...out of the Tablelands of Mexico, about four hundred years ago."

"Four hundred?" I asked. "How could an ancient culture make such an intricate piece out of black granite?"

"Well," shaking his head, "it wasn't exactly made by man—if you believe the legend. The only way I can explain it is to tell you the story from the beginning. If you got the time to hear it before Wilson gets here to kick your ass?"

"Hey!" I quickly protested, "We can handle ourselves."

"Yeah, well," Blake referred to Tony, "you'll need your fat sister to help you when you do it. He's got his own police force."

"I'm not his sister," Tony protested in vain.

"His own police force?" I asked in surprise.

"And you'll need a lawyer," Blake continued, ignoring Tony and rubbing in our problems. "Yes. Wilson told me he's got two lawmen with him and they both have brand new guns that I'm sure they're dying to shoot something. Either way, it looks like you're going to jail or the emergency room!" Blake chuckled.

I grabbed my head and leaned back in the chair in disbelief. This was getting worse by the minute and Blake was getting his rocks off just watching me squirm.

We bombarded Blake with questions and protests. The news of Wilson having his own armed police force made us lose control. It got loud quickly. Everybody was protesting and asking questions at the same time.

Blake cocked his head and raised his hands, "Stop, stop it, please. Control your passions. I'm going to tell you the story of the Black Heart Stone. Then maybe you'll be able to decide for yourselves why Wilson is on the hunt with two armed police officers."

"Is this a very long story?" Tony asked.

"Yes, but I'm going to give you the short version." Then he pointed to his library, "It beats reading everything that pertains to the stone. I have it all memorized."

We got comfortable and Blake began.

"The best way we can figure it, in the 1600s there was an ancient Mexican culture, a Mesoamerican tribe of some sort. As, they existed in what they called the Tablelands. That's in deep Mexico. They created a great and prosperous civilization that had everything a people could ask for, and they were led by a great king. All the people love him. But this ancient culture was not to remain. They were attacked by a neighboring tribe of warriors, and most of them were killed or made slaves. During this time, the king was killed, causing the remaining wise men and elders to cut his heart out of his body and use it as an offering to the sun."

"Oh, my god!" Amelia said.

I agreed with Blake, "That sounds about right. Aztecs did that kind of thing."

"Don't tell me," Tony said putting it together, "the Black Heart Stone was the king's heart?"

"Yes. According to the legend, it turned to stone," Blake glanced at us to see if we were still following him, "and it remained with that culture as their good-luck piece. As long as the heart was in their possession, they believed that their prosperity was a divine gift."

"In their possession where, Mexico?" I assumed out loud.

"No. Not exactly. They wandered the land, going north until they ended up right around here. Then the son of the king was crowned the new king, and this ancient Mexican culture built another city...and believe it or not, they prospered...again."

"A happy ending," Amelia tried to entice Blake into finishing.

"Until they were attacked a few generations later by what everybody thought were the Comanches. This time, almost everyone was killed. The remaining survivors buried their dead and the Black Heart Stone in one of their mines. Then what survivors were left went back into deep Mexico territory."

"So when do you think the stone was buried?" I asked.

Blake shrugged his shoulders and thought, "I would say sometimes in the late 1600s to the 1700s. Of course, that's just a guess."

"When was it rediscovered?" I asked further.

"In 1925, a rancher by the name of Ike Pancake found the old mine on his ranch. Inside he found the skeletal remains of a Comanche woman. He found a flint rock that had an unreadable diagram etched on it. Then he found another flint rock with the name Jim Bowie and the year 1832 also etched on it. Then last, but certainly not least, he found the Black Heart Stone."

"Wait a minute," I asked. "Are we talking about the same Jim Bowie that died in the Alamo?"

"It had to be," Blake confirmed.

This treasure hunt was getting more and more complicated. It wasn't as simple as "X marks the spot" anymore.

So I asked, "How did Jim Bowie's mark end up in an ancient mine from almost two-hundred years before that?"

"I thought Bowie died at the Alamo?" asked Tony.

"He did, in 1836," answered Blake. "Look, boys. Forget about the Jim Bowie connection or it'll drive you crazy. You've got the Black Heart Stone, so you need to stay focused on the Pancake mine. And if you want to make progress...you need to come up with the logical questions."

"Okay." I glanced at Tony and then Amelia and started to think aloud, "From an unknown Indian tribe of the Tablelands of Mexico to the days of the Alamo, till its discovery in the 1920s, till its loss in 1935, and its rediscovery today? Right off the top of my head, the first question would be why were there so many different artifacts from different time periods all in the same place?"

"That's one," confirmed Blake.

"What was originally in the mine?" Tony asked.

"Don't know," Blake answered. "No one really ever found out."

"I've got another question. How did anyone learn about the story of the Black Heart Stone?"

Blake pointed at me and smiled, "That's it. That's the right question, Luis. You're putting things together. Now, you want me to tell you where it came from?"

"Of course, I do."

Blake reached inside his shirt pocket, pulled out a folded wad of cash, and handed it to me, "Then have your maid run down to the liquor store and get me a bottle of Jack."

"I am not his maid!" Amelia told him in defiance.

"And a mighty fine-looking maid too." Blake continued to prod her, "You old enough to drive?"

We were in a quid-pro-quo situation, so I gave Amelia the eye.

She reluctantly snatched the money from my hand, "Give me that," she said and stomped all the way out the door.

"She's a very nice girl," Blake complimented her.

I just smiled and nodded my head, "Yeah. She's going to put my testicles in a vice when this is all over."

John Blake had warned us about it being a long story, and brother he was right. Every time he began to speak, he would get noticeably tense and sit on the edge of his chair like he was telling scary stories to children around a fireplace.

I had a lot of information to retain and the story wasn't over yet. At least I could take comfort in Tony watching the clock and making sure we didn't get too close to Wilson's arrival. We were trying to minimize our surprises.

"My grandfather, Frank Simmons, acquired the stone from Ike Pancake. He kept it until 1935 when a Mexican Indian from deep down in Mexico showed up at his house. The Indian and his people had been looking for the stone for at least a hundred years. They kept detailed historical records of the stone and knew everything about it."

"Did he ever say what tribe of Indian he was?" I asked.

"No," Blake answered, "Frank never mentioned it in any writings...I would have seen it if he did."

"So why didn't he take the stone back to Mexico?" I asked.

"Because when Grandpa Frank showed him that it was broken, the Indian declined to even touch it. He couldn't. According to him, it would have been bad luck for his whole Indian culture. That's when this Mexican Indian told the complete history of the Black Heart Stone. And that's it, the end to the story as I know it."

Blake finally leaned back in his chair and appeared to relax. Then he quickly sat upright, "One more thing. The Black Heart was stolen from Grandpa Frank in 1935. It's been lost until you found it. The end."

Tony slowly stood up and put his hands in his pockets, "That's one hell of a story."

I put my face in my hands and rubbed my face. I was tired. I was tired of knowing Wilson was always on my heels. I was tired of listening to such a complex story. I was tired of wondering if I was making the right decision, "So why is Wilson so all-fire determined to get this stone, Mr. Blake?"

"Beats me," Blake answered. "It's got to be worth something as an archaeological piece. It's certainly not a current religious piece. Of course, after what you've told me about him, I'd say he just didn't like you."

"You know," I said in a low tone, "when I look back on things, I just can't put a finger on how this got so personal between us."

Blake sat there for a moment and said nothing. He was thinking about something and how he was going to say it, "Say, Luis...you said your last names were De Zavala?"

I looked at him and nodded my head.

"Are you, by any chance, the descendants of Lorenzo De Zavala—drafter and signer to the Texas constitution?"

"Yes, sir," I confirmed for him. "That's what we've always been told."

"Funny. I didn't think there were any descendants," Blake said decisively.

"Why? Did you know him?" The question came straight from Tony's head. It was a small revenge.

John Blake got loud, "That would make me about one hundred and ninety years old, you damn fool! Do the math!"

This ended up being a major stop for us. By all rights and means, we would have been clueless if we hadn't stopped to talk to John Blake. Sure, we would have eventually learned about the Black Heart Stone through who knows how much research.

I knew more than anyone, but the problem was going to be maintaining possession of the stone after it was made public. Wilson obviously knew about the stone. He was surely going to apply legal pressure on me, and he knew I didn't have the money to fight back.

After Amelia came back with Blake's Jack, he walked with us all the way outside, down his steps, and to my pickup truck. That was quite an undertaking for an old man.

"What do you plan on doing with it?" Blake asked me.

"Have a big private party for my fellow diggers and show it off. It's kind of an amateur archaeological group I belong to," I told Blake in an uncertain tone. Then I became certain, "Then I'm going to sell it through an antiquities auction before Wilson can get an injunction."

Blake shook his head in agreement, "I see."

"The truth is, I have no idea what I'm going to do." I looked into his eyes, "What would you do if you were me?"

Blake patted me on the arm and said, "I'd do the same thing you said...all the way to the end and make that bastard suffer."

# 11.

# Andrew Wilson and His Two Problems (A Story in Retrospect)

I've kept in touch with John Blake concerning his uncanny approach to researching history. Blake enlightened me on some tricks that they don't teach you in college.

Years after the Black Heart Stone, I got a chance to talk to Blake during one of my visits. We sat down on his front porch and he told me the story of what happened that day after we left his house. This time I didn't have to worry about someone coming down the street to get me.

♥ ♥ ♥

"You left just in time," Blake stressed upon me. "Wilson pulled up to the house not too long after you left, and there was a second vehicle that came with him. It was those two young cops he told me about on the phone - fresh out of the academy and still wet behind the ears."

Blake told me how he stalled his conversation and kept Wilson there for as long as he could.

"I gave him a long-winded story," Blake admitted, "and I gave it to him slow."

So I asked him the obvious, "Did he ever figure out what you were doing?"

"He didn't right away, but he did later. The only reason he listened to me for as long as he did was out of respect for the elderly, I guess. He knew enough about the Black Heart Stone; he didn't need anything from me. All he wanted to know was when you left my house. When I finally told him you left about an hour prior, he surprised me. It didn't piss him off like I thought it would. The man had a lot on his mind."

"Was it me," I asked, "was I the one on his mind, you think?"

"Well," Blake thought, "kind of...but not as much as those two yahoos that came with him."

"I guess I should have tried harder," I told Blake.

Blake told me that he and Wilson watched the two young cops out of the corner of their eyes. The longer they watched them play the game of juvenile grab-ass, the more concerned they became with the safety and professionalism of the whole project.

"Wilson didn't like what he saw," Blake told me. "That much I do know. Somebody went to a lot of trouble to turn them boys into archaeological police. Their names were Barney and Beto."

All I could think of was what a waste it was. Commissioning an officer of the law for archeology was as important as hiring cops to keep the opossums out of the dumpsters. It wasn't needed because nobody cared.

Then Blake gave me the history as he knew it. He said that Barney and Beto were two want-to-be Texas Rangers, not yet fully grown and both struggling to look older than they were, which was hard for them since they looked like they were still eighteen.

The Department of Public Safety carried their peace officer commissions, which gave them state-wide jurisdiction, only answering to the department head, which was Andrew Wilson, and a DPS colonel out of Austin's central command.

They were fresh out of the Austin Regional Academy and none of their clothes fit. Everything was too loose and baggy. Beto had problems keeping his gun belt up on his hips, and Barney's cowboy hat would blow off his head at the slightest breeze.

"I must have watched his hat blow off his head three times while he was here at the house," Blake told me. "They didn't have any experience, whatsoever."

I had to add, "You know, they're gone now. Wilson got rid of them."

Then Blake told me something I didn't expect, "Doesn't surprise me. Those boys got a raw deal."

"A raw deal?" I asked.

"They weren't mature yet," Blake explained, "especially to be lawmen. No one to learn from...probably their first job of any importance. Oh well."

Blake was certainly more forgiving than I was. I thought that Barney and Beto both needed a knot on top of their heads. Blake felt sorry for them and the predicament they were hired into.

Then Blake looked at the ground and chuckled, "Still, Wilson had his hands full. It was one of the funniest things I'd ever seen."

Then he told the story of what he saw.

"While we were on the porch, we watched a puff of wind blow Barney's hat off. When Beto jumped to grab the runaway hat, his entire gun belt slipped over his hips and almost to his ankles. It was like watching little kids, I swear.

After Barney managed to catch his hat, he walked over to Beto and they started to talk to each other. Then for some unknown reason, they pulled their pistols out of the holsters and started comparing them. Recklessly waving the damn things around in the air, making all my neighbors nervous as hell. But the final straw was when they decided to have a quick draw contest. Both had shit for brains. Then it got even better."

Blake told me that Wilson finally couldn't stand it anymore. He left the porch and walked over to Barney and Beto, presumably to give them a good talking to.

"Put those things away!" he ordered them. "Jesus! You're making spectacles of yourselves."

"You know what, Mr. Wilson?" Barney asked. "One thing I've noticed is you've been on our case ever since we started this manhunt."

"Yeah. Tell us why that?" Beto asked as the second ignoramus.

"I keep telling you boys, this ain't no manhunt," Wilson tried to explain to them through his controlled frustration.

"Then why are we in pursuit of someone?" Barney asked.

"We're not in pursuit, dammit! I keep telling you that too. I need you just in case we are forced to make an arrest." Wilson took a breath and regained his composure, "Look. I'm sorry I raised my voice. It's not your fault. I wanted two close-to-retirement types. I needed experienced lawmen that knew how to do investigative research. That's all. It's not your fault."

Blake told me that for a second, he thought Wilson's yahoos understood. Wilson had put it to them in a way he thought they would understand. Evidently, there was no such luck.

"Ain't no old fart retiree investigator going to be able to run down a perpetrator if he bolts, Mr. Wilson," Barney squeaked out in his boy voice. "But me and Beto here, we could run him down."

"Or shoot him!" Beto enthusiastically added.

Wilson started losing his patience for the second time, "There is no running in archeology! Or shooting!"

"It's because of that black rock thing, ain't it?" Barney asked.

Blake told me he was up on the porch laughing his ass off at what Wilson had to deal with. He also thought for a moment that Wilson gave up because he rubbed his brow, stared at the ground, and said in a calm voice, "I'm paying for my past sins. That's got to be it."

Then, out of the clear blue, Beto recited a monologue in Spanish, *"Nunca podré entender por qué alguien nos contrataría para un trabajo y luego no quiera que estemos aquí. Tenemos posgrado. Fuimos a la academia. Podemos disparar mejor que nadie."* [1]

Barney crossed his arms and looked at Beto like he understood every word

"Of course it is!" Barney said to Beto.

Blake said Beto appeared to be in deep contemplation of some Spanish philosophical moment.

Then Beto continued to ramble, *"Se queja de nosotros, pero le vamos a mostrar. Tú y yo. Nos lo vamos a echar en la bolsa y nos darán medallas. Seremos héroes en todo Texas y conoceremos al gobernador. Y luego nos dirá que lo siente frente a todos."* [2]

Wilson looked at Barney and asked, "So? What'd he say?"

"I don't know, I don't speak Spanish. I thought you did."

Wilson shrugged his shoulders, frowned, and shot daggers through his eyes, "Get in your vehicle and go gas up. I'll be right behind you."

Before Wilson made it out of his yard, Blake said he shouted one final question, "Is there going to be trouble?"

Wilson stopped and turned around, "Take a look, Mr. Blake," Wilson told him, referring to his two new peace officers. "This is my trouble...my real problem. It's something I've been regretting ever since I inherited it."

[1.] *"I'll never understand why someone would hire us for a job and then not want us here. We both graduated school, went through the academy...we can shoot better than anyone."*

[2.] *"He's complaining about us, but we will show him. You and me. We'll eventually win him over and they will give us medals. We'll be heroes throughout Texas and get to shake the governor's hand. And then he will tell us he's sorry in front of everyone."*

# 12.

## The Chase

Traveling cross country through the small towns was a nerve-racking experience. We were all on the lookout for Wilson and his two cops. The slower speed limits and traffic lights didn't help matters either. As far as we were concerned, Wilson was behind every cedar tree and every rock along the side of the road. This made for a long and tedious day. Twenty-four hours of traveling and paranoia will take their toll on a person.

The quickest way to San Antonio was to find Interstate 35 and then turn south. Wilson might be able to run us down on the small two-lane country roads, but if we could make it to the interstate, there would be enough heavy traffic to keep us relatively concealed, making it highly unlikely that he could ever find us.

After we made it to Interstate 35, I noticed that we all let down our guard a little. Everybody was exhausted from riding in the truck, and we all knew if we pushed it any further, we weren't going to get home until late that night. By that time, we would be worthless. So I made the decision for all of us to stop in Round Rock and get a motel.

I picked a twenty-story high-rise that overlooked the city. I considered this particular motel a good risk. There were a thousand cars between us and the interstate with hundreds of businesses that ran parallel to the highway. Since everything was laid out like a maze, I thought it would be impossible for Wilson to find us.

Tony and I got separate rooms next to each other, both on the third floor. We also had the good fortune of balconies that overlooked the city of Round Rock, and the motel swimming pool was directly below the balconies. It was a nice place. We had a great view of the whole city.

After I took a good look at the city from the balcony, I went back inside and plopped on the bed.

♦ ♦ ♦

The next morning I awoke to Amelia clanging around in the room. She had made one of those small pots of coffee that the motels leave in your room and then walked out on the balcony, leaving the sliding door open. I could see Tony was already on his balcony, enjoying his own cup.

"You get any sleep?" I hear Tony ask.

"Yes, and you?" Amelia answered.

"Ah...I'm too restless for some reason," he said. "I kept waking up."

Amelia knew what Tony's problem was, "You're too anxious... about joining the army, I mean."

Tony took a sip from his coffee mug and gazed over the landscape, "Yeah. I don't have any idea what to expect, other than what the recruiter told me."

Something caught Amelia's attention down in the parking lot below and she stopped listening.

Tony kept talking, "I'll be the first one going to the service since Papa Sergio..."

"Tony, look!" cutting him off and pointing at the parking lot below. "Can you read what's on those two cars?"

When Tony looked down, he confirmed for the both of them, it was the two vehicles marked *Texas Department of Natural Resources* on the doors.

"Oh no," Tony groaned, "How in the hell did they find us?"

I had heard everything they said. I jumped out of bed like an alarm went off and looked over the balcony. Sure enough, there were Wilson's vehicles sitting in the parking lot.

"You see them drive in?" I asked.

"No," Amelia replied. "They could have been there all night."

"Not likely," Tony said.

"We need to pack up now," I said with an urgent tone.

Everyone scrambled to get dressed and pick up our few things.

Suddenly there was a loud knock on our door. The voice on the other side shouted, "Mr. De Zavala! This is hotel security! Can you open the door please?"

I ran back onto the balcony and tried to get Tony's attention by shouting quietly, "Tony! They're at the door!"

In the spur of the moment, Tony came up with an escape plan, "Swing me your bags and both of you step over to this side."

The distance between Tony's balcony and ours was only a few feet. Anybody could do it if you didn't look down and weren't too squeamish. I swung him our two personal bags and then turned to Amelia, "You go first."

"Yeah, before I get a chance to think about it," she said before stepping over to Tony's balcony.

There was a second louder knock on the door. Everybody jumped.

Tony put out his hand and encouraged me, "Come on! Let's go!"

They could see I had other plans on my face. "I'm going to buy us some time."

I grabbed the backpack with the Black Heart Stone in it and held it over the edge of the balcony rail, and then I dropped it. It fell thirty-five feet, where it ka-plopped nicely in the deep end of the pool and sank to the bottom. Luckily, no one was swimming at the time.

"What about you?" Tony asked. "What are you up to?"

"I'll meet you at the truck," I told him as I looked down at the pool. He knew exactly what I was going to do then.

"Yeah. That's what I figured," Tony told me.

"In the pool?" Amelia asked.

"They're only looking for me. They don't know either one of you," I told him. "I'll see you at the truck. If I get arrested, don't hang around."

Then for the third time, there was a harder knocking at the door, "Mr. De Zavala! Open the door!" said the voice.

I yelled at the door, "I'll be right there! Let me get some clothes on!"

"Tony!" I shouted again, "Wait for them to come into my room."

Louder and louder, they pounded on the door. I could hear them talking on the other side. It was Wilson and his two cops.

I ran to the door and rattled the lock chain like I was trying to open the door, but they caught on quickly. "Hold on," I said on the other side.

It was a matter of seconds before they ran out of patience.

I could hear the frustration in Wilson's voice, "That's enough! Open the damn door!"

When they opened the door, Barney and Beto came in first, followed by two security guards and the hotel manager. By that time I was on the other side of the balcony rail, ready to jump.

"Don't jump," Barney pleaded with me, thinking I was suicidal or something.

"Don't come any closer," I told the dumb-ass.

When everyone was inside my motel room, Tony and Amelia slipped out their door, walked down the hallway, towards the elevator, and right past my door. Like two unconcerned tourists, they were never noticed.

"Give it up, De Zavala!" Wilson ordered me.

I glanced at him, *"Adios, pendejos,"* and then I jumped.

I could hear them gasp. They didn't think I'd do it, I guess. But I did and fell thirty-five feet into the deep end of the pool. After I came to the surface for a breath of air, I could hear Barney say, "That crazy bastard jumped!"

Immediately, Beto started to climb over the balcony rail. He was going to make the jump into the pool too, but Wilson grabbed him by the arm and stopped him.

While they were looking at me, I dove to the bottom and retrieved the Black Heart. Then as fast as I could, I got out of the pool and ran for the truck. Tony and Amelia were waiting for me with the motor running.

The last thing I heard before I left the parking lot was Wilson's voice, "I know where you live, Luis."

♥ ♥ ♥

We only drove a few miles until all the traffic came to a complete stop. We were way ahead of Wilson and his bunch. It was a good time for me to get back in the driver's seat.

Amelia slightly shook her head, "Congratulations, Louie. The law almost got you...you're now a fugitive from the law."

"I didn't break any laws," I told her.

"Technically, you're right," Tony said. "The stone was a legitimate purchase. It's not a rare archaeological piece yet. We didn't have to come through any customs anywhere. He hasn't told you that you were under arrest—yet."

"Then why are we running?" Amelia asked.

"I don't know," I said as I looked out the windshield, "besides him being an asshole and wanting to ruin my life, I just don't know what he wants."

There were hundreds of cars in front of us, bumper to bumper. No one was going anywhere. Our side of the interstate was in a traffic jam, and the northbound lane didn't have any traffic at all.

When I stopped my truck on top of an overpass, Tony got out and climbed into the truck bed to stand up for a better view. He could see hundreds of emergency lights flashing about a mile away. There was a traffic accident in front of us and it was a big one.

For some reason, two big rigs had locked their front bumpers while going down the interstate. One thing led to another and they both lost control, jack-knifing their rigs and blocking all the north and southbound lanes.

The semi in the fast lane jumped over the concrete median and laid the trailer over on its side, spilling hundreds of gallons of paint. It was all over the highway and it was a big mess. So naturally, the fire department declared the incident a HAZMAT spill and halted all traffic. That meant we were stuck right where we were, in the right lane.

Suddenly, my phone rang. It was my mother.

She made it very clear to me, "Don't come home with that damn rock. You'll just lead the police to the house again."

"Okay, Mom," I told her.

"Go to Cade's ranch in Bandera," she ordered me. "They'll be less likely to crash his gate."

"Look, Mom...I'm sorry about all of this," I tried to apologize. "Does Cade know?"

"It was his idea, *Mijo*," Mom said. "Or, you could give the rock to Wilson and be done with it."

I stood my ground, "If I did, Wilson would sell it on the black market, and he'd put me in jail again."

"You went to jail?" Mom reacted as if she knew. "What about Tony and Amelia?"

"Everybody is fine. We're all good."

So why didn't I give the Black Heart Stone to Wilson? That would have been a simple solution. It was a question I asked myself every time my ass puckered from being pursued by him.

What importance was the Black Heart Stone? It wasn't made of gold or had precious gems embedded in it. It was an inanimate object shaped like a human heart, and it was broken of all things. Not even the original descendants of that ancient Indian culture wanted it back.

So why was I protecting it like it was the Holy Grail? Wilson knew as much about the story, if not more, as I did.

I'm not proud to admit it, but part of my reason was retaliation for Wilson hounding me on digs and discoveries over the years. Since the very beginning, I think my name was used much too comfortably in Wilson's classification of "the archaeological enemy of the state."

The other reason I didn't turn the stone over to Wilson was pure principle. To me, the Black Heart Stone was still sacred, venerated by a civilization four hundred years ago. If Wilson took possession of it, there was a danger that it would disappear and possibly end up on the black market. Anything could happen.

We sat in the truck and waited in the heat. My truck was struggling to keep the A/C going. Everyone was starting to get noticeably hot.

I had stopped just past a bridge overpass and had the truck in park. We were trying to chill out and relax. Then I noticed in my rearview mirror two SUVs slowly driving up the shoulder of the road.

"*Oye, vato.* We got company," I alerted Tony. "Somebody's about a quarter mile behind us, driving slowly down the shoulder of the road. Get your glasses and take a look."

Tony pulled out a pair of binoculars from his bag and stuck his head out of the window to see.

"Wilson's in the second vehicle, *Primo*," Tony said calmly. "The first vehicle has got two men in it. It must be those two Johnny laws."

"Well, you can bet they're looking for us, and we don't have anywhere to go," Amelia said in an irritating voice. "What are we going to do, Louie?"

She was right. Because of the traffic, there was nowhere to go except for one place. On my right side there was a steep slope going down to the access road, off-road of course. It was probably a thirty-degree grade and not meant to be driven on. To make matters more complicated, it was extremely muddy and slippery from prior heavy rains. I thought I could make it down to the access road, but it would be a one-time attempt, and I had to get it right the first time. Without asking for anyone else's opinion, I told everyone to hang on.

As soon as I turned off the emergency shoulder, Amelia yelled in disbelief, "You're not!"

Then down the muddy slope we went, sliding sideways at first and hoping like hell we didn't roll over. Amelia screamed in my right ear the whole time until we straightened up and reached the access road.

Barney and Beto quickly spotted us and followed down the same slope, but they weren't so fortunate. Gravity took their SUV and spun it sideways. They slid out of control all the way to the bottom until the tires finally grabbed hold of something, making their SUV roll over one complete rotation and come to a final stop upright on the tires. It all happened in slow-motion.

As I drove down the access road for our escape, Tony watched Wilson successfully drive down the same slope and stop next to Beto and Barney.

"Wilson made it," Tony reported, "but he stopped at the bottom."

Wilson rolled down his window. Then he just looked at them and shook his head.

They didn't hear a word Wilson said. As soon as Barney and Beto got out of their vehicle they began to slip and slide in the mud, trying to gain their footing.

Although I was relieved that nobody was obviously hurt, seeing them delayed by their own hands felt good. The last we saw of them, Barney had his straw hat pushed down over his ears from hitting his head on the ceiling of the SUV. Half of the brim on his hat was ripped off the crown, causing it to flop around his chin, and Beto was looking everywhere for his pistol again. As soon as they got out of their vehicle they were covered in mud and occupied with trying to keep their over-sized pants from falling down.

Wilson drove up to them with his window rolled down and saw that everyone was still in one piece. Then he ordered them to get back in their vehicle and follow him.

It took a while until Barney and Beto got their SUV started again, but when they did, it was in a muddier vehicle.

I took the back roads until there was a place to get back on the interstate. After that, we were traveling at top speed and making good time.

"We're not going to Mom's," I told them. "We're going to Cade's, but we're going the back way. Not through Bandera."

"Through Hondo?" Tony asked.

"Yeah."

"I need to pee," Amelia said for the tenth time that trip.

"Again?" I asked.

"Hey buster!" she barked. "I'll have you know I nearly peed in my pants during that roller coaster ride you gave me."

Tony started to laugh.

"That's not funny. Next time you decide to do something like that, let me know so I can at least put on my seatbelt—or jump out of the truck."

♦  ♦  ♦

We hadn't seen Wilson or his minions since they rolled the SUV north of Austin, and I was hoping we wouldn't see them again. I guessed that he went to my mother's house first, just to see if I was there. If he happened to be brave enough to knock on the door, I knew my mother would be there to give him the cold shoulder again.

Wilson was eventually going to find us, but at the moment we still had a running chance and I needed to keep stomping on his plans to stay ahead. If he caught us in the open, he could simply seize the stone on behalf of the State of Texas, and you can bet, I'd never get it back again. Government paperwork and legal maneuvers would keep it tied up in the courts until I cried "uncle" or ran out of money. Probably both at once.

If I could get the Black Heart Stone to Cade's ranch, it would be almost impossible for him to get inside. That would be the safest place to plan the stone's final destination.

"At least," I thought, "that would be the plan."

♦  ♦  ♦

The railroad tracks ran parallel to the highway all the way into Hondo, and the last leg of the trip was a straight shot, only thirty miles to Bandera.

Of course, we weren't going anywhere without stopping in Hondo for diesel fuel first. I chose the first station we came to, a convenience store on the south side of the highway and the railroad tracks.

I pulled up to the outside pump on the west of the island and killed the engine. With the sun on the horizon, this left the situation so if anyone pulled into the store parking lot and looked in my direction, they would be looking directly into the sun. The timing was right, but it wasn't going to last. In the next thirty minutes the sun would be over the horizon and it would be dark.

Tony and Amelia went inside the store to use the restroom while I stayed with the truck and pumped the gas.

Tony and Amelia walked past the station clerk towards the restroom.

Before Tony got too far the clerk got his attention, "Hey, man! The men's is out of service."

Tony stopped and looked at him, "It's out of service? Well, where am I supposed to go?"

"Go out back," said the clerk, "everybody else does."

I don't know about other places, but that's not an uncommon practice here in Texas, "going out back." Quite literally. Men can go anywhere, but if most women don't have a place to pee and a mirror on the wall, the world could come to a fiery end.

The store was going through a major septic rebuild in the back of the store and had only salvaged the use of the women's restroom before a heavy rain stopped the plumbers from finishing their project.

I watched Tony walk right back out the front door of the store and around to the back. I had a hunch about what was going on. Tony had been holding it for the last sixty miles and was under an intense calling from nature to release his backwater. Despite the pressure he was under, he had to pay attention everywhere he stepped. The ground was still saturated from the heavy rains earlier that day, and it was an obstacle course of dry spots and mud holes.

The plumbers dug several wide trenches very close to the back of the store using their backhoes. Most of them were about four feet deep, and all the trenches were full of water.

To make it even harder for someone walking in the back, the store had no lighting. It was dark and shadowy, and directly behind the store was a five-hundred-acre cornfield that stretched all the way to the backside of Hondo. All of that was to play a factor in what was going to happen.

Without warning, Barney and Beto pulled into the store parking lot, sped right past me, and parked outside of the front doors. They never gave me a second glance, so I immediately pulled out my phone and texted Amelia.

Amelia was standing in the checkout line with a few sodas and candy bars. Her phone dinged with my text about the same time Barney and Beto walked in the door. They were filthy from head to toe and were also looking to use the men's restroom, but the clerk stopped them.

"The men's restroom is out," the clerk said. "You'll have to go out back."

At the same time, Amelia read the text and her eyes widened with surprise. I'll give her credit for one thing; she had the composure to not turn around and draw attention to herself. Not that it mattered. I don't think they knew who she was in the scheme of things anyway.

As soon as I watched Barney and Beto walk around to the back of the store, a new wave of worry overcame me and an, "Oh shit" rolled right off my tongue.

I had assured Tony during the whole trip that he wouldn't be involved in any foul play that could bar him from joining the military, but I also knew this situation was going to be a temptation to his size and power.

Tony outweighed Barney and Beto by fifty pounds apiece as it was. He fancied himself a Jose Latherio type, a retired local wrestler that built his reputation from slinging opponents out of the ring like Frisbees. As big of nerds as they were, Barney and Beto were still law enforcement and they had the potential of causing Tony real legal trouble.

Tony was in the back, trying to take a whiz and not expecting a thing. Then, here came two filthy law enforcement officers who parked themselves next to Tony and started to fiddle with their businesses.

Amelia walked up to me and asked, "Where's Tony?"

"He's in the back," I told her, "You better get in the truck. We need to be ready in case he comes out running."

▼ ▼ ▼

Tony was arching an impressive pee stream into one of the watery trenches when Barney and Beto walked up behind him, completely oblivious to who he was.

Barney asked in a friendly voice, "Mind if we join you?"

"Go ahead," Tony replied.

Within seconds, all of them were filling up the same trench as fast as they could.

"This manhunt for that De Zavala cabron is about to wear me out," complained Beto.

Tony suddenly knew who they were, so he quickly shook it off, zipped it up, and said aloud, "What a relief!" Then he stepped behind them.

"Yeah. If Mr. Wilson would leave us alone and let us do our job, we could have that guy in jail," added Barney.

"You ever made an arrest before?" asked Beto.

"Nope," answered Beto. "What about you?"

"Nope. Me neither. But I seen it done on TV."

▼ ▼ ▼

I had the truck running and never took my eyes off the back of the store to see if Tony was coming out. I imagined that if he did, it would be at a dead run, straight for my truck.

"*Andale*, Tony," I said aloud. "Amelia, send Tony a text."

As soon as Amelia sent the text, we heard the alert from Tony's phone coming from the back seat of the truck. Tony left it behind.

It didn't matter though. While we were on the lookout for Tony, Wilson pulled up on the other side of the gas pump, looked me straight in the eyes, and shouted from his SUV, "Where you going?"

I didn't answer. I just floored it, leading Wilson on a short but wild-ass chase through the outskirts of Hondo, and the first place I tried to lose him was the Walmart parking lot.

♥ ♥ ♥

Meanwhile, in the back of the store, Tony sprinted out of the shadows and blindsided Barney like a football linebacker would a quarterback during a game. Barney went flying headfirst into that water-filled trench.

Beto immediately pulled his pistol like a good officer, and the weight of his gun belt pulled his pants down over his ankles again. As soon as Beto bent over to grab his gun belt, Tony snatched Beto's pistol from his hand and threw it into the trench with Barney.

Then Tony picked Beto up above his head like a Saturday night wrestler and spun him around and around until he was nice and dizzy. He threw Beto headfirst into the trench with Barney. The so-called fight was not even a contest. Tony slung those guys around like they were grade-school kids.

When Tony finished with them, there was nothing but Beto's feet sticking up in the air. Of course, Tony stayed there long enough to make sure they weren't going to drown. Incapacitated yes, but standing upright.

Try as they did, every time Barney and Beto tried to climb out, they'd slide back into the trench. It was too deep and slippery for them to go anywhere. Within a minute, all their energies were drained and they were completely exhausted.

Then there was the bigger problem they would inevitably have to face—the embarrassment of losing their pistols again, this time somewhere at the bottom of that watery trench.

Tony ran around the corner of the store, only to see that I was gone. So, without hesitation, he ran into the cornfield and disappeared into the darkness. His destination: Our fat cousin's house, Ignacio. Ignacio lived in Hondo.

Out of breath, Barney yelled at Tony as his image disappeared into the cornfield, "You're under arrest!"

"I don't think he heard you," Beto told him.

Barney was feeling around his belt, "I can't find my gun."

"I lost one of my boots," Beto added.

❦ ❦ ❦

I felt bad about having to leave Tony, but I was having my own problems with Wilson. At one point he was chasing me in circles in the Walmart parking lot. I wasn't about to stop and be apprehended by that asshole, and he wasn't about to quit chasing me, so I stayed just ahead of him. That was all I could manage for the moment.

When we finally got out of the Walmart parking lot, things got a little faster and a little wilder. My truck was hard to control when we drove on the side roads. Tony's rocks, our backpacks, and everything we had placed on the dashboard were being flung back and forth all over the inside of the cab.

I wasn't going to shake Wilson at what I was doing, and I didn't want to go into a neighborhood, so I came up with an idea.

"Put your seatbelt on," I told Amelia.

"Louie! What are you planning to do?"

"We're going to jump the tracks," I told her. "I doubt he'd try and follow us over the railroad tracks."

I knew exactly where I was going to make the jump, too. There was no natural road crossing there, just a giant overpass that went over the railroad tracks in the design of a huge cloverleaf. If you wanted to cross to the other side of the railroad tracks and be legal about it, you had to take the time to take the cloverleaf. That would take too much time and Wilson would surely stay on my tail. I was going to take a shortcut by jumping the railroad tracks and was willing to bet that he wouldn't follow me.

After Amelia clicked her seatbelt on, she looked at me with genuine worry, "I hope you know what you're doing!"

I reached down to the dash and turned the selector switch to four-wheel drive, high. Then I led Wilson on a wide loop so I could build up speed and aimed my truck straight for the tracks. We hit the embankment of the railroad tracks with just enough speed to clear the rails.

As I was betting, Wilson saw what I was doing and slammed on his brakes just in time. He was much too conservative to try the same stunt.

It was not a soft landing. It was bone-jarring, unlike the movies. I thought for sure we broke something somewhere, like my right eardrum that Amelia was screaming in the whole time.

As soon as I cleared the rails of the track, I floored it and my engine roared all the way across the muddy corner of the field until we got to the pavement of the highway. In my case, the four-wheel drive I had was crucial that day.

Totally unexpected and with her hair over her eyes, Amelia started laughing. "That was so much fun! Just like in the movies, Louie," she shouted while clapping her hands together. "When this is all over, can we come back and do it again?"

Wilson didn't have any choice but to go back around and cross the railroad tracks at the overpass. I knew this would give me enough lead time to keep in front all the way to Cade's ranch.

We slung mud all over the highway and left an obvious trail to follow. Of course, the further I drove, the lesser the trail there was to follow. I figured that Wilson would follow it as far as he could until he ran out of mud tracks to follow. Then he would stop looking. I figured wrong.

Ten miles farther down that highway and I noticed my diesel fuel gage was registering about half of where it was supposed to be. It became obvious that the jump over the tracks had put a hole in my fuel tank. I was losing so much fuel that I didn't know whether I was going to make it to Bandera or not. That meant Wilson could pick up the diesel trail I was leaving when the mud tracks quit. I was leaving a steady stream of diesel on the pavement that a blind man could follow.

I knew Wilson would pick up on this and start following my diesel leak. The chase was far from over and I was about to run out of easy options. All I could do now is convey to Amelia how serious things were getting.

"Amelia. Listen to me," I told her in a serious tone. "We're not going to make it to Bandera. We're losing too much fuel. The jump must have busted a hole in the fuel tank."

"What do you mean? We're not?"

"Put all the cell phones and the Black Heart Stone in one backpack," I told her. "We're going to ditch the truck and walk out."

"What? He'll see us walking on the highway, Louie," she smartly commented.

"No, he won't," I told her. "We're going to ditch the truck at the Medina Gravel Pit and walk out on the back side. If we head west, we can get to Cade's fence line in about an hour."

Not a single plan I made during that whole trip, went accordingly, including the incident that followed at the Medina Gravel Pit.

I was originally going to drive over the fence and slip inside where I knew the fence was laying down, but the front gate to the gravel plant was wide open. It was supposed to be closed and locked. That was my first clue that something was fishy.

No one at the pit worked at night, but I drove in the main gate anyway. Since the last thing I wanted to do was attract attention, I turned off my truck lights as soon as I turned off the main highway. I did my best to keep a low profile.

One thing that would work to our advantage was the fact that the sky was clear and there was a full moon. You could see practically everything you wanted without artificial lights. Especially when it came to the moonlight shining on the white limestone walls of the gravel pit.

With my truck lights off, I had no choice but to slow down about a half mile into the plant until we nosed off farther down into the pit area. All the limestone walls that surrounded us towered straight up about one hundred feet. It was an impressive sight to behold in the moonlight and soon to be a scary obstacle for Amelia.

As soon as I reached the basin, I could see the field shack up ahead. It was the only man-made structure at the bottom of the pit.

For some odd reason the lights were on. There were also four vehicles parked around the shack. That was the second and the third clue that should have told me things weren't normal, but I quickly dismissed it as someone working late.

"Looks like somebody's here," Amelia commented.

"Well, we're not pulling in to say hi," I told her in a much quieter voice, "As soon as I hide the truck, we're going to tiptoe around them, real quiet like...and climb to the top of that hill."

Amelia looked at the rock face and her jaw dropped, "That is not a hill, Louie. That's a cliff. I can see that much even in the dark."

"Whatever you want to call it, we got to climb it," I stated with false confidence. "Once we get to the top, it's a clean shot to Cade's. We get up high enough, I should get a phone signal and we can call him to come get us."

I slowly pulled in behind some big boulders where I felt the truck would be hidden well enough and then killed the engine. No one was going to see the truck from the road, but I felt certain that Wilson would eventually find my truck because of the diesel trail it left. By that time, we would be long gone into the wilderness.

Amelia and I snuck right past the shack and up to the base of the rock wall. We could both hear people talking inside, but we kept quiet and kept walking.

Amelia looked up at the wall and whispered as loud as she could at me, "Oh no! Louie! I can't do this. This scares the shit out of me."

I turned around and tried to shush and calm her, but it was too late, "Keep your voice down. This is no time to be wimping out, Amelia."

Amelia sat down on one of the rocks and started to hyperventilate. "I'm going to vomit," she said most convincingly.

"No, you're not going to vomit!" I commanded her. "Here! Give me your pack. I'll lead the way. You put your foot where I put my foot, your hands where I put my hands."

"Maybe you should go without me and I'll give myself up to the authorities," she said as the bravery was leaving her body.

So I knelt down beside her, "Listen to me, sweetheart. Anyone who can let a thousand spiders run all over her body and not hardly complain about it can climb a little rock hill. Hell, Theresa would be so proud of you...being a rancher's wife and all. You're nearly there."

Then she stood up and took a couple of deep breaths, "Okay, you're right. Maybe I can do this. Yes. I can do this."

So up the hill we went. Halfway up the face, the reality set in and she started to whine with fear. I could hear it all too well and did my best to counteract her fear. That's also when I was the most worried about things going really wrong. The thought of her losing her grip and falling was absolutely terrifying to me.

Amelia crested the top, but not without the sounds of grunting and growling that went with the effort. When she reached the top, I thought she was going to start shouting in victory, but I'm glad she didn't. Instead, she did her own little happy dance to celebrate.

We had the advantage to watch Wilson drive up to the field shack with his lights on, park his truck, and go inside.

He did exactly what I thought he would. He followed the diesel trail all the way to my truck. When he didn't find us in the truck, he walked to the shed where the lights were on. It was a bad decision.

For the next three minutes, we didn't see or hear anything. Then, without warning—and I mean without *any* warning—here came the police, swooping down like a bunch of hungry owls after the last rat in the barn. Eight police vehicles and probably ten officers surrounded the shack to make sure nobody could escape.

This wasn't the FBI or the DEA. This was the DPS Narcotics division, and they had been staking out the shack the whole time. As far as anyone knew, they had officers hiding behind every rock and dark spot in the area, waiting for the right moment to pounce. How Amelia and I ever went through there without being detected can only be attributed to our stealth in the darkness. They might have later had questions about my abandoned truck in the pit, but for all practical purposes, they never knew we were there. As a result, we got to see the whole show from the top of the gravel pit.

"Looks like we made it out just in time," Amelia sighed but looked concerned. "Poor Mr. Wilson. I hope he's okay."

"Yeah. Poor Mr. Wilson," I said, trying to sound compassionate. "Maybe now this will take him out of the picture, permanently."

She looked at me in the moonlight and asked, "Surely you don't wish him any real harm...do you?"

Before I could answer Amelia, a helicopter arrived in the area, shining its light on the perimeter of the scene.

I slung the backpack with the Black Heart Stone over my shoulder, "Let's get out of here while we still can."

As Amelia and I walked into the darkness of the cedar and towards Cade's ranch, all I could think of was how I was finally rid of Wilson. He had caused me so many problems with his skewed ethics, and I felt a great relief when I saw him arrested, even though I didn't know what he was arrested for. As I found out later, the only other person that they didn't arrest was a man that they dearly wanted, and his name was Tomato.

▼ ▼ ▼

We crossed several property fences that night. We had to climb a few more hills too, then crawl through some thick brush, but Amelia never complained again. Climbing that rock cliff in the dark was a big jolt to her confidence.

"How far to his property line?" asked Amelia.

"About four miles, give or take some," I told her. "The most important thing is that we get there before the moon sets on the horizon, then it'll get really dark."

We reached Cade's high-fence before the moon went completely down. I had a phone signal, so I called Cade and we waited there and leaned on each other until he showed up in his truck.

We were both very glad to see my *gringo* friend and his wife

Theresa when they pulled up. Amelia and I were both exhausted and dirty from our ordeal. Of course Cade made sure the ice chest was full of cold drinks to help alleviate our pain.

"Cade, I'm worried about Tony. I had to leave him," I told him with regret in my voice.

"Tony's fine. He called right before we left the house," Theresa informed us.

"Thank god!" Amelia said with relief. "We were worried the cops got him."

"The cops? What cops?" Cade asked.

"He called from Ignacio's house in Hondo," Theresa continued. "Then he called Anna to bring him a set of clean clothes."

"I want to see that Black Heart Stone; see what all the fuss is about," Cade said.

The questions they asked were expected. While we were running across the state of Texas trying to dodge the authorities, they were all worried sick about our welfare.

"I'll tell you all about it on the way back to the house. First, I need something to drink," I assured Cade and then downed the first soft drink I got my hands on.

That night we all stayed up late talking about our adventurous trip. Then we broke out the Black Heart Stone and tried to answer all the details they asked for. Amelia had everyone captivated with her enthusiastic play-by-play descriptions of events. I had a lot of fun watching her tell the stories. It made me rather proud of her. Never had I seen that side of her before. She was now an exciting character of exuberance.

I tried to be happy for my so-called victory, but I caught myself pretending instead. No matter how hard I tried to be upbeat, something was wrong and I wouldn't admit it. Things weren't right by a long shot.

It's easy to tell a story once the danger is gone and you're in the warm safety of a home, but the whole ordeal unexpectedly left me with an unresolved issue. My conscience was bothering me.

For the first time in my life, I feared losing what integrity I had. It's not like any person sat me down, shook their finger in my face, and gave me a good talking-to. I can only describe it as a lesser haunting, made from the inaudible whispers of the men's shoulders I stood on. It was a guilt that came without fanfare or explanation. It was like I had betrayed someone's trust, and I knew deep down it was something I had to fix.

I needed some good advice. I needed to talk to my Papa Sergio in the worst way.

# 13.

## Shallow Victory

The next morning, we called everyone in our Texas Artifact Diggers club that we had the phone numbers for. That was about one-hundred people. Once Cade got on the internet and put the Black Heart Stone's story online, everyone wanted to see it while they still could. Everyone also knew that the future of an artifact like that would be uncertain. It was a matter of "see it while you can."

My mother, Anna, wanted to have this viewing of the Black Heart Stone at her house, especially since Wilson would most likely still be in jail. Of course, she insisted on having food and drink for everyone. She was a natural at entertaining.

♥ ♥ ♥

We had a lot of arrowhead diggers show up at the house the next day, and everyone seemed to concur—the discovery of the Black Heart Stone was a significant find. Of course, the bonus was getting Wilson out of the way of our digging group's efforts.

About lunchtime, Mom turned on the TV to see if there was anything on the gravel pit incident in Hondo. There was, and it was an eye-opener. It was the number one local story of the day.

"The Director of Archeology for the State of Texas, under the Texas Department of Natural Resources, was arrested by DPS Narcotics in a drug trafficking bust," said the reporter.

Wilson was still in jail.

I couldn't watch the whole report. I had to walk away.

Meanwhile, everyone in our digging group that came to see the Black Heart Stone was thoroughly impressed. We got to tell the story over and over again.

At the end of the night, there were just a few people left standing around. I was burned out from the excitement and found myself tuning out every conversation that came my way. All I wanted was to be alone. My attention span was gone.

When I thought no one was watching, I walked into the kitchen and sat down by myself. That's exactly where I wanted to be. I needed some uninterrupted time to think.

Before long, Theresa walked in through the door. She went to the kitchen counter where all the food was and piled a second helping onto her plate.

That's when it hit me, I had never seen Theresa come back for seconds before. She wasn't really interested in more food on her plate. She had something to say to me.

"You want to talk about it?" she asked.

"Talk about what?" I said, trying to play dumb.

"You know, all those people out there? They all love you. They also know you, Luis. And they can tell when something is wrong," Theresa told me.

Like I said before, Theresa was the smart one of the bunch.

I glanced around the kitchen not really knowing how exactly to begin, so I took a deep breath and did my best, "I can't shake this feeling of being responsible...the guilt that I feel..."

"Professor Wilson?" she confirmed with a question.

I nodded my head, "Maybe. I don't know. Wilson did that to himself!"

Theresa sat down across the table from me and stared at me. There was heavy sarcasm in her voice, "Of course he did, Luis. Everybody's *always* suspected Wilson of being a big drug dealer anyway! Right?"

"Come on, Theresa! You know what I meant. It's not my fault

the man's in jail."

"You did all you could do," she said, again patronizing me. "You're innocent."

"Innocent of what?" I blindly asked. "So why do I feel so, bad about this?"

She stopped eating and looked at me seriously, "It could be that bad feeling you have is a residual effect on a man with a conscience. What do you think?"

"I think I need to talk to Papa Sergio."

Then Theresa told me her main point, "You know what I think Papa would tell you? I think he would say that you and Wilson need each other, like two quarreling lovers."

My eyes widened at that one. "Surely, you're kidding?"

"Who caused you to run such a fantastic obstacle course across the state of Texas while protecting the Black Heart Stone—a prize that no one knew existed until it was rediscovered? I know people that would have paid a lot of money for an adventure like that."

"I never had a choice. He's been after me for years," I replied.

She pointed her fork at me, "He's been keeping you at your best, Luis. I say he's made you a better archaeologist."

"Think so?" I asked.

Theresa was nibbling at her food like she wasn't interested in eating. I could tell she was about to give me a big speech about something. If she wasn't so damned smart, I would have told her I wasn't in the mood, but she was that smart, so I listened.

"About ten or twelve years ago, a well-known archaeologist out in the Houston area by the name of Fulmer claimed to have found the knife of Jim Bowie. The actual knife that was taken at the fall of the Alamo."

"*The* Bowie Knife?" I asked, pretending to be in the know, "It was thought to have been taken back to Mexico by one of Santa Anna's soldiers."

"By coincidence," Theresa continued. "Dr. Know-It-All Fulmer, as I called him, was also good friends with our past governor,

Governor Bark Smith. And, he was friends with the then director of Texas Archeology."

"Of course," I pessimistically said, "That's how political corruption rolls, and I'll bet the director was Andrew Wilson, wasn't it?"

"Nope, it wasn't. It was a man by the name of Ned Collier, Doctor Ned Collier," she revealed to me. "Oh, Wilson worked for the department all right, but at that time, he hadn't been there even a month. He was a college new hire that worked in the back rooms. All he did was classifications, and nobody ever saw him. As far as the big-wigs were concerned, Wilson was a nobody."

"So, who authenticated the knife?" I asked.

"Governor Smith's "yes man" Dr. Fulmer, of course, and the Director of Texas Archeology, Dr. Ned Collier," she said. "The classification was a foregone conclusion, and they knew no one would dare challenge their findings - so they thought."

"Wait a minute!" stopping her before she continued. "Of all people, I should know about this. That knife is thought to be in a private collection somewhere in Mexico."

"True enough, Luis, but there's more to the story." Then she continued, "Before they went public with the discovery, they decided to have a private party for themselves. It was an exclusive invitation, made up of various archaeologists, senators and congressmen, daughters of the republic, movie stars, sons of the pioneers—as far as I knew anyone that was anybody was invited. Behind those closed doors, they all got a good look at that knife...then they proceeded to drink themselves stupid."

"That doesn't make any sense," I told her confidently. "If the knife existed, I would have known about it."

"And you want to know why you don't?" she asked, "It's because a rather small and pimple-faced young man, fresh out of college, managed to sneak in and crash their party."

I looked at her and silently hoped I was wrong, "Wilson?" I asked.

"Yes, Wilson. While no one was paying any special attention, he managed to get a good look at the Bowie Knife. One of the congressmen noticed what he was doing and asked him what he thought about it. Wilson looked at the senator with a long face and replied, "It's a fake." And that caused the shit to hit the fan.

Andrew Wilson was immediately confronted by what turned into an angry mob. He pissed off the whole herd of dignitaries to the point that I thought they were going to get a rope and lynch the poor guy."

"You were there?" I asked her.

"Yes," she told me. "I was doing an internship with the Capital News as a reporter trainee while going to UT-Austin."

I was surprised, "I would have never known. You a lady reporter!"

Then she slightly lowered her head, like she had lost something, "I was prettier back then, and had more faith in our system. Nobody cared if I could write or not. They cared how short my skirt was. I got so fed up with everything that I was about to give it all up and come back home when one of our state senators invited me to that party. I couldn't pass that up."

"You show up in a short skirt?" I asked, trying to push her buttons.

She glared at me, "Yes I did. But to get the story, there was the condition that I swore not to publish anything until the actual press release date about the knife."

"What happened to Wilson?" I asked.

"The next day Governor Bark Smith had Director Ned Collier fire Wilson."

The profile Theresa painted of Wilson confused me, to say the least. This wasn't the profile of the Wilson I knew. What kept me focused on my disdain for him was what I did know. Now what Theresa was telling me made me think maybe it was only what I thought I knew: the scoundrel, the skunk of the highest order, the sophisticated embezzler that stole precious artifacts and sold them for money. I still had my separate list of violations, but the longer she talked, the more questions popped into my head. I had to know more.

"So then what?" I blurted out. "Wilson's the director now. How did he get there?"

"There was one political rival of Bark Smith that looked into the authentication of the Bowie Knife. His name is John Maxwell."

I raised my eyebrows, "You mean our now governor, Johnny Maxwell?"

"Yep. Same guy," Theresa confirmed. "Before Wilson could clean out his desk, John Maxwell invited two Louisiana archaeologists to Austin and re-authenticated the knife—and threatened Governor Smith to go public if he tried to stop him. Collier couldn't say "no" either. His ass was on the line and so was the reputation of Dr. Know-It-All Fulmer. And guess what happened? The Louisiana archaeologist agreed with Wilson. The knife was a fake.

When Governor Bark Smith got the news, he knew he couldn't run for a second term. Maxwell would have drug him through the mud. And I believe he really would have."

I assumed the rest of the story, "And Johnny Maxwell was elected to the governor's mansion...Andrew Wilson was reinstated? Is that how it happened?"

"Pretty much," she said. "When Governor Maxwell won the election, he fired Collier and re-hired Wilson to take his place. It was an act of political revenge. Then Fulmer was discredited and run out of town. Bark Smith never ran for office again."

I took a deep breath, leaned back in my chair, and sighed, "It doesn't negate the fact that he skims off the top of these discoveries, Theresa. I've been watching him for years. Every time he's involved, something ends up missing."

"Okay. Did you ever actually see him do anything, Luis?" she asked. "Were you actually there?"

"No. Not exactly, but I'm not blind. I inferred these clues to reach that conclusion." I thought my logic would put an end to the cross-examination, but it didn't seem to faze her in the slightest.

She pointed her finger at me, "That's not proof, Luis. If you're wrong, you've been falsely accusing him."

I pretended to be thinking about it since she had me frozen in place. It was just as I predicted, she hit a home run right over my head.

"No wonder Cade never wins an argument with you," I said. "You're some kind of evil psychologist. Aren't you?"

She kind of laughed and then started to pick at her food, "You know? I was fortunate in my upbringing. My father, my brothers, my uncles...all good men. If there's one thing that I learned from them: you don't have to be smart to do the honorable thing. But if you do, it builds you as a man."

Theresa never told me directly what I should do. Her message, however, was clear. And she was right. As bad as I didn't want to hear it, she was right.

●   ●   ●

The next morning, I was the last one to get up and out of bed. Cade, Theresa, and Amelia all spent the night at the house. I could hear everyone in the kitchen, clanging around with the dishes and getting breakfast ready. The smell of *chorizo*, the sound of bacon frying, and the smell of coffee meant I was in heaven.

In the background I could hear everyone's voices as they sparred with one another for fun. It occurred to me how fortunate I was. I was home with the family I loved. All the money in the world couldn't buy what I had.

I walked through the doorway into the kitchen, cleanly shaved and dressed for business. Everyone turned to me and stared. No one said a word.

"I won't be eating anything just yet," I told them. "I've got some unfinished business to tend to first."

They knew what I was about to do. Mom was the first one that came up to me and hugged my neck. Then Amelia and Theresa grabbed me, both hugging and kissing me until they started to tear up. Both of them were afraid that something could go wrong and I could end up in jail again.

Then Tony and Cade shook my hand.

"Hell of a brother, you are," Tony told me.

"We're going to be waiting for your call, Luis," Cade promised.

I left the house with one defined mission: to set the story straight about Wilson's involvement and hopefully get him out of jail. I didn't know the intricacies of criminal law or how to navigate its system. All I knew was that I had to do what I could.

# 14.

## The Act of Integrity

Those two narcotics investigators looked at me like I was crazy. After all I told them, I could see that my story wasn't sinking in.

After a few minutes of staring at me like I was a two-headed dog, Investigator Number One leaned back in his chair and asked, "Let me get this straight, De Zavala. You're trying to tell us that the department head of Texas archeology, if there is such a thing, chased you halfway across the state of Texas to get a four-hundred-year-old rock that also happened to be a man's heart?"

"Yeah. Something like that."

"That's a pretty wild story," Investigator Number One commented.

Investigator Two asked, "There's one thing I don't understand. If he was what you said, such an enemy, then why would you go through so much trouble to get him out? You know he was busted with a bunch of other scumbags. He was right in the middle of the shit."

For just a half second, I broke eye contact with the investigators and slightly lowered my head, "I don't know that he ever was my enemy."

"You could have fooled me," Investigator One said.

Then I caught a second wind, raised my head, and spoke up a little louder, "Look! He's always been a pain in my ass, but he's not a drug dealer! He's an archaeologist."

It didn't occur to me that breaking eye contact might have been a mistake until later. I'm just glad I finished with a louder bark than when I started. Those boys were professionals, criminal investigators able to read a person's mind by watching every intricate facial expression and body movement that was used. I was out-skilled in this department, and I knew it.

"I think it was more a matter of truth and honor," I finally told them, not knowing how they would interpret that explanation.

"Well, hell! We can understand that," Investigator Number One said with a straight and confident stare.

"This has been fun, but I think we're done here, De Zavala," Investigator Number Two told me trying to wrap up the interview. "Do us all a favor and stay by a phone. We may want to talk to you again."

Oh well. I did what I went there to do. The rest was up to them. My only contingency plan was that I'd try to talk to the district attorney about the case if Wilson wasn't released.

I even had thoughts about getting a lawyer or contacting the press, ACLU, or somebody that could help. And although I went through the steps accordingly, I am ashamed to admit that my heart still wasn't in it. I was only there because I had that inner feeling, compelling me to be.

While I was still outside the steps of the county jail, I sat down on one of the benches. My emotions were drained and I needed a few minutes to get it together. After about thirty minutes, I decided that I was good and stood up to leave.

"Luis! Luis De Zavala!" said the shouting voice of Professor Andrew Wilson, "Hold up for a minute!"

Wilson shuffled down the steps of the jailhouse and walked up to me. That was the first time we had ever met each other person to person.

Wilson gathered himself and thanked me, "For what it's worth, Luis, thanks. They told me that it was you that set the record straight."

I was not impressed nor swayed, so I maliciously threw salt on a convenient wound, "It's more than you ever did for me."

"Yeah, well, I feel bad about that, but if you knew what I was doing," Wilson tried to explain, "you'd know I had my—"

"Save it! Please, save it," I interrupted him in a disrespectful tone. "I did what I came here to do. You're out of jail, now do me a favor and leave me alone."

I tried to immediately walk away, but a moral wave overcame me and made me stop in my tracks. I probably made it ten feet. The truth was that no man like Wilson deserved to be talked down to like I just did to him. I belittled him to his face only because I could. I was in the wrong and I knew it.

The only honorable thing to do was to turn around and make things right. When I did, Wilson was still looking at me, not knowing whether he dared to say anything to the man that got him out of jail.

I slowly walked back up to him, and as hard as it was for me to do, I offered him my hand to shake and lowered my tone, "Mr. Wilson. I apologize. I had no right to speak to you in such a disrespectful manner."

After we shook hands, Wilson started to point aimlessly and gesture back and forth from me to him, "How did we get here, you and me? I don't understand how we got to be such frivolous enemies."

Surely Wilson wasn't as clueless as he was acting, or maybe he was trying to piss me off?

My volume went immediately went back up again, "The ninth keg to the Salado Spanish cache? You have any idea what everyone thinks?"

Wilson raised his voice in a defensive tone and stood toe to toe with me, "No, Luis! I try to make it a habit not to come to conclusions over stupid-ass rumors! What are you, some old woman? Why don't you do us both a favor and tell me what everyone thinks? Go ahead! I can't wait to hear it!" he asked.

So, I told him exactly and bluntly, "You sold it for yourself on the black market and pocketed the money."

He angrily pointed his finger in my face. "That's bullshit and you should know better!" he demanded.

"Do I? It seems like every time you do one of your archaeological seizures, something ends up mysteriously disappearing. That's why

137

we dread you coming around."

Wilson waved his arms around in a gesture, "I can see things have got way out of hand."

"Now you're after the Black Heart Stone, aren't you?"

Wilson looked at me and emphasized, "No, I'm not." He squared his shoulders and asked, "Take a good look at me, De Zavala. Look into my eyes and tell me, do you think I stole those things and sold them on the black market?"

He was giving me the perfect opportunity to accuse him of theft and profiting. He was giving me an open opportunity to call him a liar. I immediately realized the weight of an accusation like that and I balked, not knowing what to say. I couldn't make myself say it.

"I don't know Mr. Wilson. To tell you the truth, I have a hard time believing a man in your position would ever do something like that. Then, I'm still reminded about the cases like that ninth keg. Can you see my problem?"

Wilson nodded his head and looked at his watch, "I tell you what. I need something to eat. That jailhouse food is terrible. You let me buy you lunch, and I'll tell you what happened to the ninth keg— and the other missing items that you think just disappeared. You'll be the only one who knows."

"Really?" I confirmed.

"Well...you and the governor."

After an offer like that, I wasn't about to say no. He was offering me the chance to walk into his inner sanctum. Good or bad, I had to find out.

♥ ♥ ♥

We went to a local restaurant that was well-known for its steaks and seafood. Wilson chose an isolated booth on the far side of the restaurant, kind of out of the way from the other customers.

It didn't take long until we ordered, and then Wilson immediately plunged into the buttered bread they brought out and laid on the table.

"I take it, you didn't eat very well while in jail?" I asked.

"Just enough to stay alive," he responded.

As soon as Wilson got a few pieces down his throat and wiped the crumbs from his hands, he took a breath and looked at me across the table.

"It was no picnic," Wilson explained, "I can tell you that much. But the alternative was that the cartel would have had me eating dirt by now."

"What exactly happened when you went inside that shed?" I asked.

"You were watching?" he asked but didn't seem surprised.

"From the top of the gravel pit...in the dark," I revealed.

"Well!" he said and picked up his glass of tea. "This is what happened.

When I walked into the shack and closed the door, the first thing that hit my senses was the smell of marijuana. Not marijuana smoke, but raw harvested marijuana right out of the fields. It was all neatly baled, packaged, and sitting in the middle of the floor.

I only had a second to regret going through that door, when four rough-looking dudes walked out of the shadows carrying guns— and they weren't on a dove hunt. I was in the wrong place at the wrong time. Believe me, they were armed to the teeth."

"What'd they say?"

Wilson continued, "The head honcho asked me if my name was Tomato?"

"Tomato?" I asked.

"Then they all stared at me. I could see they were disappoint- ed, and that made me real nervous. You see, Tomato was the name of their contact, and it didn't take long before they figured it out. I wasn't Tomato."

" 'This ain't Tomato,' said one of the drug runners, 'this guy's a stray.' Then he asked me, 'What do you want, *Guero*?' "

"To keep from being tortured and killed, I decided to put my hand on my wallet and ask if I could buy a couple of joints...if they could spare it, of course."

"That was an original. No doubt," I said.

"It didn't work either. They knew I didn't belong there. They just stared at me and let me contemplate my own death. Their business was large volumes, enough to make a man rich and dead in the same night."

"You were lucky," I told him, to fill the void of what was to come.

Telling him he was lucky was a frivolous comment. It was almost an insult to his intelligence. That caused Wilson to stop talking, squint his eyes in anger, and look into the distance.

"Let's get to the meat and potatoes, Luis," Wilson said with force and conviction. "I don't appreciate being accused of things like theft, especially when it comes to my life's long work, the preservation of antiquities!!"

Wilson was going to understand something early about me, I wasn't going to be someone he could push around. I was going to be just as combative as he was.

"Fair enough," I barked back at him. "Skip the bullshit then and enlighten me. I'll tell you what I think when you're finished."

I knew I wasn't making relations better between us, but for the time I let my hostility stand.

The way he looked at me across the table, he was trying to size me up. He might have had thoughts of changing his mind and not telling me anything. However, I'm glad he did, because what he was about to tell me would change everything between us.

"You know where that ninth keg went?" Wilson asked.

I shook my head.

"I sent it back to Spain as a gratuitous gesture," Wilson revealed. "The same can be said for every discovery I can legally seize for the state. In the long run, I keep Spain from taking us to court on a claim. Spain's always glad to get something back if they can avoid a court battle."

"Why haven't we heard about this in the media?"

Wilson pointed to himself and stopped eating for a moment, "Because I'm the department head, the director of archeology. I alone make policy. If there was a written policy, then it would be subject to the Texas Open Records Act, allowing all the public to see."

"Wouldn't that be a good thing?" I asked.

"No. I tried that before and it always turns into a giant mess. I tried to publicly announce some of the returns in the old days, and every morning after, a truckload of legal writs would show up at the office, all claiming some kind of ownership. Those cases take years to get resolved. That's why now I keep it quiet."

The waitress brought us our food. That gave me a chance to think about my next question.

"Does the State of Texas know what you're doing?" I asked.

"Like I said, only the governor—and he understands. He's an old arrowhead digger from way back."

So I gave him a test question, "Let me ask you something. You believe there was a curse on King Tut's tomb?"

"Yes and no. As an archaeologist, it doesn't really matter," he stopped eating and looked at me. "What matters is how I treat a venerated object, something of religious significance...with reverence. But that's the second reason I do this."

"My grandfather warned me and my brother about that very same thing a long time ago," I told him. "I had no idea anyone else did too."

"You know who's behind the Black Heart?" he asked but answered his own question. "Thousands of souls that have never found a place to rest. The only thing they can connect to here on earth is what they remember as mortals, the stone. And they'll protect it if need be."

"Pay homage or there could be consequences," I added so he would know I understood.

"That's right," Wilson confirmed for me. "Call it a curse or hex or whatever. Did Blake tell you about the Pancake farmer that mysteriously died?"

"No."

"Well, let me tell you. In the late eighties, two farmers were plowing a field next to the Pancake Mine when they unearthed one of the Indian skeletons that was obviously buried on site after a Comanche raid." He leaned in over the table to emphasize his point, "That was three hundred years ago, mind you. One of the farmers thought it would be funny and took the skeleton home in a box so he could show all his friends. That night he died in his sleep. No lie."

"Holy shit, Mr. Wilson. You're right, I didn't hear about that one. Was he sickly by any chance?"

"Do me a favor, Luis. Please stop calling me Mr. Wilson? I'm just a few years older than you. Call me Andrew, or Andy."

"Okay," I gladly accepted. "You know, we have our bylaws in our digging group. No grave robbing, no desecration of sacred sites. We have our ethics."

"That's good to hear," he said with a sense of relief, "you know the modern tomb raider is secular-driven. They only care about one thing...making money, no matter how many graves they have to step on."

"No one teaches ethics in college," I proclaimed. "Maybe they need to?"

"That's a good idea!" Wilson agreed. "It's not like digging up some dinosaur. Upsetting spiritual guardians can bring down the shit. If those atheistic bastards keep up their raiding and selling on the black market, they're going to cause more laws to be passed. We've got too many now."

"Ain't that the truth!" I agreed with him again.

We were on a roll, conversing with each other in a steady flow. All that agreeing with each across the table was unfamiliar to me and quite unexpected. I had a good ten seconds to think about the next thing that came out of my mouth while he was eating, and I thought it was the right decision.

"You want the Black Heart?" I asked. "I'll give it to you if you want it."

Wilson stopped eating and looked at me, "No, I don't. Never did. But I'd like to catalog it for documentation."

"I don't want it, Andrew," I confessed. "All it's done is wear me out and make me churn an ulcer. Something bad could have happened to any one of us, but it didn't. I'm thankful for that, but I just don't have the desire to keep the thing any longer. It's been a burden ever since I've had it."

I could tell by the look in his eyes, he never expected me to make him an offer like that.

"I tell you what," Wilson said, "you keep it for a while and think about it. Just let me take some good pictures before you decide what you're going to do with it."

There was still the situation with his two cops and Tony. As far as I knew, they had no idea who Tony was. I wasn't going to tell him the whole story, but I had to probe.

"You still have your two archaeological policemen?"

"When I get back to the office, I won't," he assured me. "They're not worth the trouble. It was never my idea in the first place. I only did it to make the damn governor happy."

I was glad I took the time to eat lunch with Andrew Wilson. I learned a lot, and now I respected the man. You might say that we parted as friends. Of course I had to assure him I wouldn't reveal his systematic practice of returning portions of the treasures.

The best part of that day was getting to shake Wilson's hand again before we both went our own ways. I apologized more than once about my behavior. We both left with a mutual understanding of each other. As it turned out, I was just as much of a mystery to him as he was to me.

# 15.

## Establishing Everyday Life

My passions in archeology were the actual digs themselves. I loved to get in the dirt and feel the thrill of digging up the unblemished arrowhead. I also liked the research part that it took to document these artifacts, always preferring the work it took to get there more than the glory and fame that came with the recognition. That's why when I decided to donate the Black Heart Stone to a museum, it didn't bother me in the slightest.

Professor Wilson helped me decide what museum it would be best suited for. One thing was for sure, the ancient Indian culture it came from didn't want anything to do with it. We contacted them about it, and they basically said in their own language, "Hell no! With all of the ghosts hovering around that thing? You got to be kidding?" It was still considered a bad luck charm since it was broken.

Even after three-hundred years of being hauled all over the country, stashed in the Pancake mine, and lost "who knows where" for all that time, they weren't even curious enough to want to look at it.

Wilson got his pictures though. He did a write-up on the Black Heart Stone in some magazines, and I helped him with it. In the end, he added my name to the article we wrote. He made sure my name was on a national archaeological publication that came out quarterly. This made me a legitimate and recognized archaeologist throughout the state of Texas. It was a big feather in my hat, and I couldn't have been more grateful.

The Black Heart Stone was kept at an undisclosed location for about six months. After all of the close examinations of the stone were finished, officials shipped it to a museum in Austin.

🔻 🔻 🔻

Several weeks went by. I felt the burden lifted from my shoulders. Putting the Black Heart Stone in a proper place was one of the most satisfying things I ever did, and unforeseen by me there was to be a ripple effect concerning my actions.

When all was done that could have been done for the Black Heart, my mother called me on the phone one day. She had received a certified letter from the Texas Department of Natural Resources, Department of Archeology, Professor Andrew Wilson.

"Do you want me to open it for you?" Mom asked me.

"Might as well," then I started to hold my breath. "I just hope it's not a lawsuit or something."

I could hear Mom make quick work of the envelope in her hands. She read it to herself and then told me, "*Mijo*, you have been offered the position of assistant director of archeology by the Texas Department of Natural Resources."

I about shit my pants. That was totally unpredicted. I had to hear more, "You have got to be kidding, Mom! Who signed it?"

"Your number one enemy, Professor Andrew Wilson."

I knew exactly what I wanted out of this letter, but I had to give some thought and talk to Amelia first. I didn't want to make a mistake on this.

"Do me a favor," I asked Mom, "put the letter away for safekeeping. I'll come by later to get it. I need to talk to Amelia."

🔻 🔻 🔻

Tony joined the army without any problems. Somewhere during his training, he realized that the army was better than he expected. He fit right in and became a combat engineer like he said he would. Mom was happy for him until they sent him to Iraq. Then she started to worry. Iraq was always in the news, and it seldom made good headlines.

In 2012, Amelia and I were married at Papa Sergio's ranch. It was a good day. We made it a simple outdoor ceremony and put a big emphasis on lots of good food and cold drinks.

Papa Sergio got quite a kick out of our wedding being held there on his little ranch. Even though he was ninety-two years old, he turned out to be a big hit with the younger crowd.

Cade was my best man, and there were no problems. That is until Amelia's maid of honor showed up and recklessly sprinkled her pheromones all over my groomsmen. Then the well-planned and orderly wedding fell apart.

Juanita was from the same clan that Amelia came from. I think her expertise was casting spells on the weak-minded of the opposite sex. On the day we got married, I watched her walk down the aisle and cause a five-groom pileup like wrecked cars on a busy highway. Of course she was built like a Michelangelo goddess too.

♦ ♦ ♦

I was finally married to the girl I loved. In our early days, Amelia and I were very optimistic about our future. Like most newlyweds, we were driven by our combined hopes and dreams that most married couples strive for.

Amelia and I rented a house in Devine, a town just west of San Antonio. I took a job at an outdoor recreational store, and Amelia took a job at a flower shop. It wasn't much of an accomplishment considering I had to look at my diploma on the wall every morning. It was, however, a daily reminder of the possibilities for a better future. First things first. I wanted to start my family.

We spent a lot of time with family from that point on. Life was good, but I never seemed to make enough money to do anything except pay the rent and make the truck payments.

I tried to ignore it, but barely making it month to month bothered me. My hopes of buying that boat I always talked about, taking Amelia on a trip, or especially saving the family ranch gradually became a distant memory. As time went on, it became more of a fantasy than anything - out of reach and unobtainable. Not having enough had an effect that gave me a bad attitude. This problem became to fester, and the guilt of my inadequacies was slowly starting to show.

The one that saw my change first was Amelia. She was a natural in the personalized rescue business. She had a gift for reaching into another person's soul and plucking them out of the darkness. When she did this, you could watch her put her entire heart on the line when it came to other people's needs.

Over a period of time, I became complacent and bored with everyday life until it affected my everyday activities. It showed for the first time when I picked up a daily habit of drinking after work. First, it was a beer or two after I got home. Then it became four or five. Sometimes, I would drink so many I'd forget to eat supper. Amelia tolerated it for a short period, and then she did something about it.

One day after work, Amelia walked up to me while I was in the backyard staring at our solid board fence. From my back door to the back of the fence, it was only about fifty feet, and there was nothing there to look at. Literally nothing but brown grass. I was trying to figure out where my promising future had gone.

"Louie. Look at me."

I turned around and asked, "Hey, Sweetheart. Is it time for dinner?"

"Listen to me. Tomorrow is Saturday, and we need to go see your grandfather. Your mother told me he's starting to forget things. We need to go see him while we can."

Amelia was right about seeing my grandfather. A visit was long overdue. Besides, after a talk with Papa I always left a better man. Although I went to see him more than anybody else, it never seemed enough. As for my other cousins, well let's say, they didn't come around unless there was something in it for them. They thought their lives were too busy doing other important things.

♦ ♦ ♦

I found Papa Sergio at the barn, trying to dig a new hole for a fence post. His work was obviously slow, but hey! I'm sure he was the only ninety-two-year-old man digging holes in Texas at the time.

"*Oye!* Papa. Let me do that," I told him and grabbed the post-hole digger from his hands.

"Look who's here! One of my long lost grandsons," he said as he leaned on a shovel. "That's my last hole. I've already done twelve."

I grinned at him, "You know what they say, timing is everything."

"Where's Amelia?" Papa asked.

"She's inside I guess...probably cleaning up the house or something."

He looked in her direction and nodded his head, "You married well, *Mijo*."

I stopped digging and stared at the hole for a few seconds, "Lately I've been worried about keeping her."

Papa acted surprised. He gestured to the house and asked in a higher pitch, "You got trouble at your new house? You barely been married."

I leaned on the post-hole digger and looked at him, "No. No trouble. I'd do anything for her, Papa. But a girl needs nice things...a little luxury every once in a while. I've been working my ass off, and everything I make goes to bills. I can't even take her out to eat. One of these days she's going to get tired of that shit and leave."

Papa looked around and thought about it, "Leave to what and go where?"

"I don't know. Some *sancho* with more money, I guess."

"If you fall over from your sad story, fall in one of these empty holes so I can cover you up while I still have a shovel." He started to chuckle, "You don't believe in yourself, *Mijo*...and your wife? She is like your grandmother, she is."

I gazed over at the house and smiled, "Yeah?"

"Every new family that goes through hard times and survives is twice as strong as the family that never had any problems. You know? When your grandmother and I were married, we had nothing. No inside toilet, no running water. No electricity. Your grandmother washed our clothes outside in a big bucket."

"I never knew that," I said. "Sounds like you lived through some hard times."

"Si, hard times. But very happy times. Your grandmother and I had a passion for each other. Together we could not be stopped. You," pointing at me, "should see your hard times and embrace them. Do not be afraid."

"I can do it, but I think Amelia will draw the line at washing clothes outside in a bucket."

My real father? I never knew him. He mysteriously disappeared from the family before I was imprinted with his image. There was no one else I could talk with when it came to "man things" except Papa Sergio. He was one part of the family that really cared about his grandkids' welfare. He always gave the best advice.

I know it's hard for some people, especially the emerging generations, to take advice from a ninety-two-year-old man that's covered in wrinkles and walks with a slight limp. There are those that are too impatient to listen and learn from their own grandfathers. Papa knew things. Tony and I believed him when he said things and we always did our best to take his advice.

"You are still a young man," Papa told me. "You have many adventures to live, and remember this...a man that has lots of money is not rich. He is just a man with money and many problems. What you have in your heart and in your family makes you rich."

I stopped digging and looked at Papa, "I need to write all of this down."

"Better days are coming, *Mijo*. You watch and see."

My grandfather had more faith than I did in that respect, but I was learning fast. The fact that I always took the time to stand there and listen till the end was an accomplishment. I left with a full heart.

♥ ♥ ♥

About a week down the line, I took out my largest box of arrowheads and poured them out on the kitchen table. It was time to sort them out and do some classifications. Then, if I could make some handsome arrowhead displays, I could probably sell them for some extra money.

After an hour of cleaning and separation, Amelia walked in from the living room carrying that big Bandera history book. She stopped at the door jam, looked down at the open pages, and asked me, "Louie, do you know where Cade's family got the money to buy that big ranch he lives on now?"

I stopped working and thought about it, "I don't know. I think he inherited it or something."

"Do you know what Cade's grandfather did for a living?"

"How would I know that, Amelia?"

"Okay. Was he, by chance, a doctor?" she asked further.

I looked up and thought about it for a second, "Could have been."

Amelia turned the book around for me to see the picture she had her finger on, "Take a look at this, Louie."

It was the reprint of an old black-and-white photograph of two men standing next to an old one-engine airplane with no farrows.

"That's an old picture, all right," I commented. "Who is it?"

"Doctor Bill Ferguson," she said. "This picture was taken in the 1940s."

"Cade's great-grandfather?" I asked.

"Maybe."

Then I took a closer look at the other man in the picture, "And the *vaquero* standing next to him? Who is that?"

"It doesn't say."

"Bill Ferguson, the doctor?" I commented, but I didn't really care. The truth was that I was more interested in sitting back down to continue my arrowhead cleaning.

"There's one more thing." She thumbed to the back of the book, where she had previously bookmarked a page.

"Listen to this," she continued. "Further on in the book, there's a news article that came out in the *San Antonio Express-News*. They re-printed it in this history book, and this is what it says - Doctor Ferguson died in a one-engine plane crash in Bandera County on August 10th, 1948...and that's about it. Again, there's no first name. You think this is the same Dr. Ferguson from earlier, or is either one of them Cade's grandfather?"

"I'll have to ask him. Don't you have any good news in that book?"

"It is what it is, Louie. It was a long time ago, you know? I try to imagine myself in the old days and what I would have done. All the hardships and setbacks? A traveling dentist in the Texas Hill Country? That had to be a first...probably took them forever to find a replacement. I don't think we have one now."

The part about the dentist got my attention. For the first time since the Black Heart Stone, I sat there with my mouth hanging open, speechless, and looked at her.

"He was a dentist?" I asked with caution.

"Yeah. A dentist."

Amelia had no idea what she had accidentally unraveled. My only question was if this was the same doctor that had crashed in the golden Eagle Warrior incident, and if it was, why didn't Cade ever tell me the story?

# 16.

## Reagan Canyon Part II — 2015
## Brewster County, West Texas

As futile as my efforts had become, I made myself face a grim future. "It's not going to be long before I am dead," I thought to myself.

The misery index was so high that it suppressed any panic I was capable of. Being so weak from what the desert had done to me, I lost the incentive to claw my way out of that predicament. And the last act I remembered was asking God to not let me go out that way.

Then my mind drifted in and out of consciousness like a spirit between two realms of existence, at times to see my own body from above, lying there motionless on the ground and wondering how odd the picture was. And how odd it was that I could still hear things around me.

There was the sound of a vehicle in the distance. Not highway noise, but more like the sound of a truck running across the desert. It could have been from Mexico or from the north. I didn't have a clue. Then everything went black. Again, I drifted out of existence and into a dark place for—well—I can't say how long.

When I came to, Andrew Wilson had my head in his hands and was slowly dribbling water into my mouth. It was those dribbles of water that had brought me back to life.

It is also worth noting, it was Andrew Wilson that warned me about crossing the river and going into Mexico. He was my supervisor and I worked for him.

♥ ♥ ♥

A few years before the Reagan Canyon incident, I picked up that registered letter he had sent to my mother's house with the job offer in my name. After I thoroughly examined it to make sure it wasn't a hoax, I talked it over with Amelia and then accepted the position: the assistant director of archeology for the State of Texas. With my degree in archeology and extensive experience in site excavations, Andrew Wilson managed to move me straight to the top within a very short time.

The money wasn't much to brag about, but it was more than what I was making before, and it was one of the best moves I ever made for my career. I was happy and so was Amelia. Andrew let me keep an office in San Antonio while he worked out of Austin.

♥ ♥ ♥

"No big gulps, Luis," Andrew told me in a soft but controlled voice. Then he placed a sopping wet rag over my eyes so I could recover my vision and dribbled more water over the other parts of my skin, "I'm going to cool you down slowly."

Then I heard a different voice that was with Andrew, "Professor Wilson! If you want to, I'll call for a medevac helicopter and we can get him to a hospital a little sooner."

I grunted out, "No," and tried to shake my head so they would get my point. The way I saw it, I had already been too much trouble. I didn't want to be any more.

"That must be my answer," the voice said. "Take your time getting him rehydrated. I'd hate to see him foundered before we get him back to town."

"Thanks, Bob." Then Andrew spoke to me, "Luis, that other voice is Bob Dunlop. He's a special cattle ranger for the State of Texas. He was the only one that had enough smarts to know where to look."

While the wet rag was still on my eyes, I managed to gravel out my appreciation, "Thanks. I owe you."

Bob kept looking towards the south for something. There was nothing obvious to see, but he still answered me, "When you get recovered, you can buy me a cold beer. We'll call it even."

When Andrew took the wet rag from my eyes, my vision was relatively restored. The only side effect was a blurry halo around everything.

Bob Dunlop was a Special Texas Ranger for the Texas and Southwest Cattle Raisers Association. He was more flamboyant than the other Texas Rangers I had met. Standing at over six feet, wearing a big thick mustache, wide brim hat, western vest, and a high-rise shooting rig for a single-action revolver, he looked like a wild west character right out of the history books - the typical image of the western lawman. Of course, that could have all been for show too. As far as I knew, he couldn't hit the broad side of a barn with that fancy pistol of his.

Law enforcement didn't typically dress like Bob Dunlap. Everyone else was more conventional, donning uniforms for particular departments. But the single-action revolver as a service weapon? That was the kind of service weapon used in the 1800s and unheard of in today's modern law enforcement.

Cattle rangers were generally allowed to set their own policies, just as long as they never embarrassed the Texas and Southwest Cattle Raisers Association. However, when it came to legal matters, they answered only to the District Colonel of the Department of Public Safety. They could do just about anything they wanted because there were no stringent policies to make them walk a line.

The Cattlemen's Association and DPS left Bob alone. He earned his privilege because he had two untouchable skills that no other law enforcement officer would dare challenge him on.

The first one was that he was an exceptionally fast and accurate shot with that single action of his. He had a quick draw technique that regular law enforcement discouraged. Conventional law enforcement considered it an unsafe practice. However, Bob constantly practiced this method until he was a master at it, leaving observers dizzy every time he drew his pistol.

Every shooting range with pistol competitions feared his name on the rosters. All the Border Patrol, Texas Troopers, and other local law enforcement dreaded being out-shot by Bob. He unwittingly mocked them by dressing like a John Wayne character from a western movie and carrying a 45 single action on his hip. He was fast and he was accurate. And he would gladly take your money in a shooting contest.

Bob's secondary skill was the fact that he was a better tracker than any Border Patrol agent or any government trapper in the Alpine sector. Countless incidents of "lost and found" and "tracking down bad guys" proved that without a doubt. There was no question about it. Bob Dunlop the real deal.

Ranger Bob Dunlop would come into my world, save my ass, fade back into his world, and then resurface again years later because of an infamous incident that was to happen in the Big Bend area. And my brother Tony would be involved. But that is another story for another day.

I looked up at Andrew and squeaked out a dry question, "How... you found me?"

"You never called in," Andrew explained. "And I had a hunch. Bob here...well he convinced me that we needed to start looking before it got dark."

I turned my head and looked at Bob. He was staring across the desert to the south. He looked interested, but we couldn't see if he was looking at anything or not.

Then it was time for me to apologize, "I'm sorry, Andrew," almost crying. "I'm sorry I crossed the river. I know you told me not to, but I did it anyway. All I wanted was something cold to drink, Andrew... but they took my ATV and ran me out of town."

"Don't worry about it, Luis. You're back in one piece, that's all that matters."

"Those assholes wanted to kill me," I told him. "I don't even know why."

"Don't tell me," Andrew guessed. "A small looking adobe *cantina* with a bunch of cold beer signs, just on the other side of where the water is really shallow?"

"Yeah. How'd you know?" I asked.

"Cause I been there," Andrew revealed to me. "That's why I know not to cross the river. I went over there once and they gave me the same kind of reception."

"How'd you get away?"

"I had to fight my way out...put all six of them in the hospital," he told me with a semi-straight face.

"Really?"

Bob started to quietly chuckle in the background.

Andrew poured some salt packets inside a water bottle and shook it up before giving it to me, smiling, "No, Luis. Not really."

I liked to see that side of Andrew. He wasn't all business, you might say. He could be full of shit like the rest of us.

Bob lowered his binoculars and said, "Somebody's coming in a jeep."

"Well, that's just great," I complained. "I guess they took the long way around. I just don't understand why they want me so bad."

Bob put the binoculars back up to his eyes, "You saw something, evidently."

"I don't have any idea what it could have been," I tried to explain.

"Drugs. Everything they do over there is connected to drugs in some way or another." He lowered his binoculars and looked at me, "You weren't involved in the drug thing, were you?"

"Not a chance in hell," I answered confidently.

"Well then, don't feel so bad. This is not the first time a man was lured in by a flashy cold drink sign. It's happened before."

I was regaining my strength fast, enough to blurt out, "I don't want to be the cause of this! Can we get the hell out of here?"

"No can do. I know these old boys," Bob told us while he was walking to his pickup truck. "They got a destiny to fulfill, and I am here to make sure they get there."

Bob took a 12-gage shotgun from his truck and gave it to Andrew. "It's fully loaded," he told Andrew. "If things go south, use this shotgun. Aim for the center of the body."

Andrew took the shotgun from Bob, but I could tell by the look on his face, he wasn't happy about it.

Bob walked about fifty yards and stopped to meet the jeep. He was wearing his single shot colt 45 in his holster and a second tucked in reverse on the left side of his gun belt. There were three men in that jeep. For just a second, I thought this was going to be an unfair fight, and I was right. The *pachucos* in the jeep should have brought more men.

When they stopped their jeep and all three of them got out, Bob was already in position. With one foot slightly forward, he was in the Weaver stance, or as others called it, a staggered stance.

It looked fairly simple. Bob was ready to fire his pistol just like he was shooting targets at the rifle range. What the Mexicans couldn't fathom was those two guns Bob was carrying on his gun belt were more akin to two bolts of lightning.

All three Mexicans had a total of three handguns and two assault rifles that everyone could see. For the moment, they were smart about it. They weren't pointing the guns at anyone, yet.

Bob spoke to the head man in the most disrespectful manner he could muster, "Where's your passport, Ochoa?"

Ochoa, spoke first, "I no need a passport. I go where I want, Dunlop."

"Not over here, you don't. You want me to call the Border Patrol for you, check you in proper?" Bob asked him.

Then Ochoa pointed my way, demanding, "We want that *hombre.*"

Bob immediately replied, "You know the way things work around here. You can't have him!"

Ochoa stated his reason, "He shot Pedro."

"Lie," I said.

"Well, that's different," Bob said with a sarcastic tone, "maybe the some-bitch will die."

Bob's "doesn't give a shit" attitude didn't surprise Ochoa. He'd had dealings with Bob before. I'm sure Ochoa knew that the only reason he was still upright was because Bob willed it, but Ochoa never got a chance to tell his two *compadre* bodyguards to be careful, and those boys looked way too nervous.

"You are one man," Ochoa said in an attempted bluff. "We are three."

"There won't be when I'm done with you," Bob told them without hesitating. "Think about it."

And they did. They thought about it for about fifteen seconds, which for their sake wasn't long enough.

So, Bob gave them a second chance, "I'm giving you the chance to get your ass back across the river while you're still able."

The tension of the confrontation was too much for the youngest of Ochoa's men. He was too young to have acquired any discipline, so the last mistake he made was when he tried to raise his AK-47 at Bob.

In the blink of an eye, Bob pulled his 45 and shot him in the right lung. Before that man even hit the dirt, Bob had re-holstered his gun and was back in firing position again.

Ochoa immediately reached out and placed his hand over the remaining man's gun. *"No te muevas,"* he told him, making sure he didn't do the same foolish thing.

"How bout it? You want to go for two?" Bob shouted and dared them.

The man that Bob shot wasn't dead, but he was badly wounded. In fact, even from my position behind the truck, I could see foamy blood bubbling out of his chest wound. Ochoa and his men were in an instant predicament.

"Okay! Okay! No more shooting. We go back," he told Bob.

They picked up their wounded *compadre* off the ground and loaded him in the jeep.

Before they left, Ochoa yelled at Bob, "We be seeing you again!"

"I'll be waiting," Bob told him one last time.

The whole incident nearly gave me and Andrew heart attacks. I was sure glad we finally got out of there, but more importantly, I was sure glad Bob Dunlop was on our side.

♥ ♥ ♥

They kept me overnight in the local hospital to make sure I didn't have any long-lasting effects from the heat stress event I survived. According to the doctors, I was lucky.

Yes, I was lucky, and I knew it. So, as I promised, Andrew and I invited Bob Dunlop to dinner on one of the last nights we were in Alpine. I was determined to buy him a cold one like I had promised.

Bob Dunlop downed his first beer without taking a breath between gulps. I'd never seen a man drink a beer as fast as that. When he finished, he placed the glass on the table and looked at both of us.

"You know? I've been thinking about something that might shed a little light on the situation over there. You ever heard of the Billy Kelly Mine?"

"Sure...as a legend," Andrew answered.

"Well. Not too long ago a pair of our undesirable *gringos* grew some wild hairs and crossed the river at Reagan Canyon." Bob continued, "From what I heard, they dug holes all over the other side of the river and made a general mess of that side."

"They find anything?" I asked.

"Don't know. All they got for it was themselves dead. The Border Patrol found their bodies. They were drug to this side of the river by the cartel...no explanations." Then Bob looked at us, "You think that was the Billy Kelly mine they were looking for?"

"Hard to say," said Andrew. "Nobody knows anything about the Kelly mine. Everybody that could have told the story is dead. All eight of them. With your story, that would make ten."

I looked at Bob and came to my conclusion, "They thought I was looking for a damned gold mine? They almost got me."

The moral of the story kept coming up time and time again. There is a price to pay when pursuing riches under the banner of the impure heart. This was something that Papa Sergio warned me and Tony when we were kids. We never forgot it.

As of today, King Tut's remains are on display in a museum.

The entire civilization of modern man won the battle to display his sarcophagus in museums around the world, but not before the lives of men were taken by its curse. That was the price to be paid.

# 17.

## The Echoes of Drums

I liked being an archaeologist. Over time, I became quite involved with the state archaeological excavations we did as well as the ones we sanctioned. I liked the research involved, especially those that always had an interesting story attached to them.

As far as a profession goes, I couldn't have asked for more. My office was in San Antonio, and I liked my boss, but before long I noticed that my life was being consumed with archaeology. "Enough was enough," I told myself. There was more to life than just digging in the dirt all day. I wanted a home life.

After work became routine, each day I found myself anxious to go home and be with Amelia. When I did, everything from the office was put on the shelf and I became her husband. A good one I hoped.

We eventually bought a new house in Devine. Everyone told us it would be a good investment in the long run. Besides, we didn't want to live in a rental house any longer than we had to. Then the cost of living went up so fast that I was forced to start paying attention to the finances again.

It was kind of puzzling to me. All the neighbors around me seemed to be doing fine. I never recalled them complaining. So I assumed that it was just one of those things and ended up accepting it as normal because I didn't know any better.

Despite the small things, I was content with life. One day I came in through the back door of the house and expressed myself in the manly way by coming up from behind and scaring the shit out of Amelia while she was peeling potatoes.

"Ah!" screamed Amelia. "You stupid *pendejo!* I think I peed my pants."

She promptly threw a potato at me, stomped out of the kitchen, and into our bedroom. Maybe what I did was a little juvenile, but what the hell! If this was the extent of our problems, we were doing good.

So, on my quest to be the good husband, I finished peeling the potatoes while she changed her drawers.

Later that night she served steak with a big glob of mashed potatoes next to it. Stuck in the mashed potatoes and sticking up into the air was a piece of something that was the length of a toothpick. At first, I didn't know what it was. It looked like one of those nose strips you buy at the pharmacy to make you breathe better, but I really didn't know.

"What's this?" I asked as I pulled it out of the potatoes, "Some kind of temperature gauge...a PH strip?"

"It's a urine strip from a home pregnancy test," she told me while watching for my reaction.

I knew exactly what she was trying to tell me.

"Are you pregnant?" I asked and hoped she said yes.

"Uh-huh," she confirmed.

What could be better news than that? A celebration was in order. I did the husbandly thing and smothered her in kisses. After all, we were going to have a little De Zavala running around the house.

Amelia announcing her pregnancy was good news and I played along with it. Of course, my secondary wonder was if I had any urine in my mashed potatoes. So when Amelia went around the corner to get something from the kitchen, I put my nose right up to the mashed potatoes and gave it a good sniff just to make sure. From what I could tell, it was all potatoes.

From that point on, my first thoughts every day were of my unborn child and the hopes and dreams that I and his mother would wish upon him or her.

My secondary thoughts were more of a concern. How was I

going to feed the new De Zavala? After all, I was the husband and soon-to-be father.

* * *

Saturday morning the phone rang and Amelia picked it up. It was Mom and she had some confusing news.

Tony had flown back home from Iraq on a thirty-day leave and never told anyone he was coming. Instead, when he arrived at the San Antonio Airport, he took a cab to Mom's house and had the driver drop him off a few blocks from the house. He wanted to take his time and slowly walk the remainder of the distance for his own readjustment of coming back home.

Although my mother was happy to see him come through the door, she was also startled.

"Tony is not his regular self," she told Amelia. "He acts like he's sleepy all the time or something. He never called me to tell me he was coming. He just walked in the door."

"He never called us either," Amelia told Mom. "Is he home now?"

"No," Mom told her with obvious sadness. "He got in his old truck and went to see Papa."

That was all I needed to hear. Something happened with Tony in Iraq. Of all the stories we had heard over the years, the ones about soldiers returning from war with post-traumatic problems were the most disturbing. There's no way to place your finger directly on a problem like that and say, "You are now healed." It doesn't work that way.

Amelia said she didn't think she could help either. Post-traumatic stress disorder was a known residual from the carnage of war. Sins so deep and egregious, common men can seldom fathom the violations committed against each other.

No one wanted Tony's cheerful character to abandon his spirit, but if anyone could alleviate the demons he had collected, it would be Papa Sergio.

Tony had thirty days before he had to report back to the army and probably back to Iraq for his final year.

I didn't want to push things. It was only after a phone call from Papa Sergio that we went over to his house to see him. A fresh visit to Papa Sergio was due anyway.

♦ ♦ ♦

That Saturday night we sat around the campfire at Papa Sergio's. It was the same exact campfire that we sat around when we were kids. Staring into the glowing coals of a fire tends to free the mind of all the man-made worries a person can accumulate during his working hours in life. I thought Tony needed the campfire with his family. It always did me good.

We talked about everything, but nothing came up about Iraq. Then Amelia and I retold the story about when she was covered with Daddy Long Legs spiders.

Tony finally joined in, "They got a spider over there - it's so big it makes our tarantula look like a gnat. The first time I saw one, it was so big, I thought it was a crab."

"How big?" Mom asked.

Tony put out his hands and made a circle of about ten inches, "About that big. Big and harry."

"I couldn't do it," Amelia shuttered. "I can't even handle the thought of Daddy Long Legs anymore. Not five hundred, anyway."

"Can they kill you, I mean, are they poisonous?" Papa asked.

"I don't know," Tony replied. "I wasn't going to pick him up to find out. That was for sure."

"De Zavala's can't die from spider bites," I spouted out without thinking. "We don't die from minor things like spider bites, rattlesnakes, lightning strikes, crabs...swollen prostates."

Mom stood up, "Swollen prostates? Really *Mijo*?"

"Prostate health. Very important, Mom," I explained like I was an expert. "A man could lose his ability to hit a target when he pees, you know. Or even worse, he could say goodbye to his sex life."

"Aren't there supplements or something you can take to fix that?" Amelia asked.

"They don't work," Sergio told everyone in an old gravelly voice. Then he gave us his experience, "You go to the doctor and he puts his finger up your ass!"

"Oh my god, Dad!" Mom protested.

Sergio continued, "My doctor had big fingers too."

Mom tried to stop him, "No details please!" She pretended to put her fingers in her ears.

Then Papa turned up the bullshit knob too high, "One day, I think he left his ring on when he did it." He momentarily paused and looked at me and Tony, "Take it from me, my advice is to count those rings on the doctor before he starts."

"That's it!" Mom threw her hands up in the air and interrupted, "I still heard it, even with my fingers in my ears! I'm going to the house."

All of us men were chuckling at the story as Mom walked away.

Then Amelia rose from her stump, "Luis, if you ever have a prostate problem, let me know. Maybe I can fix it first," then she walked to the house.

Tony looked at me and smiled, "Hell of a woman you got there."

I put my right hand over my heart and told him, "That's true love, Brother."

It didn't take long before things got quiet. Things were not the same, and all of us could sense it. Our fun and games around the campfire were replaced by wondering who was going to talk next. The problem was obvious, but Papa and I were afraid to say anything aloud. What we really wanted was for Tony to open up and tell us about Iraq.

Then Papa Sergio asked, "Did you get to do any engineering projects while you were there? You know, build bridges and things like that?"

Tony was poking around at the fire with a stick he had picked up. He raised his head slightly and smiled at Papa, "Some."

That looked like an opening, so I had to ask, "Did you ever get to shoot your gun?"

This time Tony never raised his head. He just muttered an answer into the fire, "Yeah," like he was ashamed.

Then back to staring at the fire, making us confused by the silence that followed. You could tell he struggled.

Then he spoke up, "Look, I guess you can see it. Bad things happened over there, but I just can't talk about it right now. Not yet. So please, don't ask me."

"Whatever you say, Tony. I don't know how we can help, but let us know if we can," I told him in support.

"Tony. One question." Papa Sergio leaned towards him, "How do you see it...the family name?"

Tony raised his head and smiled. He knew exactly what Papa Sergio was asking, "It's good Grandpa. The De Zavala's are good."

I changed the subject, "You want to go on another West Texas rock hunt?" I asked.

"Not really," Tony answered with a laugh.

"Tomorrow, we're going to Cade's. Want to go?"

"Yeah, I do," Tony answered.

Before we left for Cade and Theresa's ranch, I told Tony what Amelia had accidentally found in the Bandera County history book and the questions it raised. Tony immediately became just as interested as I was. The story of the flying dentist that died in his own airplane crash was now fresh in both of our minds, as were the smaller stories that were attached to it.

The following day we went to see Cade and Theresa. It wasn't very long before we all sat down in the living room and began to talk about what Amelia found in the county history book.

"Was your grandfather a doctor?" I asked Cade.

"Yeah," answered Cade. "He died way before my time. Nobody ever talked about him very much. I don't know what kind of doctor either. He could have been a horse doctor for all I know."

My cell phone rang and nobody paid it any attention except Amelia. She picked it up, walked to the next room, and answered it for me. Our conversation kept going.

"Could a doctor in those days make enough money to buy a big ranch like this?" Tony asked.

"I don't see how. He was pretty young when he died." Cade looked up in the air thinking, "Who knows where he got the money. Maybe he was a train robber or something..."

Amelia walked back into the living room and interrupted us, "Everybody hold it! Stop." With a sad face, she looked at me and Tony, "That was Anna on the phone. Your mother said that Papa has died."

🔻 🔻 🔻

Everyone knew it would happen someday—when was the only question. All the family lived in a state of denial, growing up and believing that since he appeared to be a ten-foot-tall force of nature, he could never die.

The funeral was held in Pleasanton, Texas. We also buried him there at the local cemetery.

Cade and Theresa, Andrew Wilson, and a large group of the archaeological diggers also came to the funeral to pay their respects.

People from all walks of life showed up at the funeral. Many that nobody knew except Papa. We had a lot of personal support.

After the graveside services were over, they politely got in line and filed by the family, shaking our hands and briefly talking to us about the man they knew, Sergio De Zavala.

It was one story after another, of how it was in the old days when cowboys could still push livestock hundreds of miles on horseback before ranches fenced everything off.

One *vaquero* told a story of how Sergio saved him from certain death from a rattlesnake bite. Another on how he and Sergio hauled hundreds of cattle to the Union Stock Yards every year. They told us of the many years they rode horseback together, tending to cattle, sheep, and goats when the country was still semi-wild.

Then there were the stories of what a great negotiator Sergio became on behalf of the Mexican American community, making sure that the *gringos* wouldn't take advantage of the lesser educated. Whether it was livestock, land, personal disputes, or even once, the ownership of a dog, he became their champion.

I never heard those stories before, and Tony and I were thrilled to listen.

Papa Sergio was born in the mid-1920s. Ironic that it took a funeral to make us realize that he was a long and thick book that needed to be read someday.

There weren't that many people that came to the funeral from Papa Sergio's generation. Most of them sadly had passed.

Our biggest surprise was probably when Tony and I were approached by two old *vaqueros*. They had to both be in their eighties and looked well-traveled. Their skin was wrinkled from years of wind and sun, their stature small. Most people would consider them "small men" at first glance. Both were from a long line of *vaqueros* that seldom had enough to eat while they were tending or pushing herds of livestock. So in turn, they never had the opportunity to gain much weight. Every day they were always working and always hungry.

Tony and I immediately recognized them as being of the old-time *vaqueros*. It was part of our cultural training and inheritance.

The two men that stood before us were the perfect images of *vaqueros* from yesteryear—a proud and distinct class of Mexican American cowboys, well versed in any livestock and the expertise of a master horseman.

Their names were Juan and Anselmo, and they knew Papa since they were all kids.

Tony and I were talking to a group that started out around eight people. As they weeded themselves out from the conversations and decided to go home, Juan and Anselmo inched themselves closer to us. They wanted something.

Neither of the *vaqueros* said very much until the last person decided to leave. At the same time, Tony tried to break away and get back to help Mom with some things, but Anselmo grabbed him by the arm and gently stopped him.

"Please, senior Antonio, don't leave," Anselmo said. "We have been keeping a story about your grandfather. It has been a secret for seventy years. It is time we tell you the story."

"You must know the story of how Sergio once saved our lives," Juan concluded.

So I spouted out, "What'd he do, pull you out of quicksand or something?"

"No," replied Juan in absolute confidence. "He killed two people."

Tony looked at me and raised his voice, "Oh! If Cade were here, I know exactly what he would say...I got to hear this shit!"

"Are you sure you got the right man?" I asked them, getting a little confused. "All our lives we've known Papa as the wise and gentle grandfather type."

"Yes. He was wise," explained Anselmo, "but he was in the army, and he was not afraid of evil."

While Tony walked over to tell Mom to go home without us, I escorted Anselmo and Juan to a big shady oak tree where they could tell their story in comfort.

Anselmo did most of the talking. Neither of them smiled during the telling, and they seemed to have trouble making eye contact with us during the entire story. Such was the subtle proclivity of once ancient Spanish tradition. Or, there was something about the story that they were ashamed of.

Anselmo gazed at the horizon and tried to recall what happened.

"I think it was around 1947, spring. Sergio hired me and Juan... and eight other young boys to help push three thousand sheep from a ranch in San Diego to the auction barn at Hebbronville. We had six days to finish until we went back to school."

That got my attention. I asked, "You were still in school?"

"Si," Anselmo admitted. "Juan and me...eighteen, maybe nineteen. The other eight were younger. Your grandfather, Sergio...he was about twenty-two or three, I think."

"Child *vaqueros*?" I commented in amazement.

"Three thousand sheep is a lot of wool. I don't think I've ever seen that many sheep before," Tony commented.

My curiosity ran amok with a flurry of more questions, "What'd you do about all the cross fences? There had to be a hundred."

"How far was that?" Tony added.

Juan put out his hand to slow us down and get our attention, "Listen to Anselmo."

Anselmo continued, "Some of us carried guns. You know, pistols on our belts. They were only .22s, but good for snakes or coyotes or something. You know Sergio!"

Shaking his head, "I don't know. He carried something much bigger."

"It must have been a .45," I said. "He liked the .45."

Anselmo looked at me and nodded, "On the second morning, we woke up to the smell of smoke. There was a fire somewhere in the north. And Placido and Miguelito were missing. Sergio put Juan and me in charge of the herd while he went to look for Placido and Miguelito."

"What about the fire?" Tony asked. "Did it get any closer?"

"Yes. That afternoon the wind blew hard from the north," Anselmo continued. "Just as it was getting dark, the smoke was thick. The sheep ran in five different directions. We did our best to keep them together, but we could not see. Then the night came."

"Papa wasn't there?" I asked.

"No. Not until later that night. But first came the headlights through the darkness. It was a truck with two grown men."

"Who was it?" I asked.

Anselmo turned his head and looked at Juan. Anyone could see that he didn't want to tell the rest of the story. It bothered him.

"It was two men from San Diego," Juan said. "They worked for a corrupt, rich *gringo*. All the *gringo* ever did was take from the people."

"A bad guy," Tony said. "What did they do?"

170

"They jerked Anselmo and me off our horses and took our pistols," Juan said with a hint of shame. He lowered his head and continued, "Then they took us to some old house nearby. They tied our hands together and made us sit on the floor. They began to drink and...humiliate us. As the night passed, in their drunkenness they told us they were going to do the same to us as they did to two others that day."

While Anselmo kept his head down, Juan raised his and looked straight at us, "I'm not going to lie to you. I was afraid. We were both afraid."

"Placido and Miguelito?" Tony asked.

*"Como?"*

"Was it Placido and Miguelito the *banditos* were talking about?" Tony tried to confirm.

*"Si,"* Juan answered. "Sergio found them before the fires came."

Anselmo couldn't stand to hear the story again but was compelled to say more, "They were violated!"

"Violated?" I asked, making them get a little bit more specific.

Juan spoke up, "Those men took their horses and they took their saddles...and then they violated them. Sergio found them curled in little balls, like newborn rabbits laying in the brush. Placido and Miguelito were...not in their right minds. Sergio took them to a house that he knew."

Anselmo spoke up, "We did not know what happened to Placido and Miguelito until later."

"What about you?" I asked. "What happened?"

Juan continued, "Those men became *muy borracho*. Then there was the sound of someone walking on the porch—the sound of boots and spurs walking to the open front door. I knew by the sound of the rowels, it had to be Senior Sergio.

One of the men said, "Sounds like it's George. The Duke himself." But the man that walked through the front door was Sergio, and he looked different. In his left hand he carried a lit cigarette. The bottom of his vest was tucked into his gun belt. And out for everyone to see, his pistol was sitting higher than usual with the hammer strap off.

Sergio stopped inside the door and cocked one leg, *'Oygan cabrones.'*

The two men stood up to confront Sergio and one of them said, 'Who the hell are you?'

'I'm the guardian angel...to the boys you had your way with today!' Sergio told them."

"The two men looked at each other and then reached for their guns." Juan explained further, "Sergio killed them both. Every day I am thankful for what he did."

"Our grandfather the killer," I commented.

"No!" Juan insisted. "He was not a killer. He was a righteous man."

"Of course he was," I acknowledged. But I still had more questions. "What about the loose ends? Like the bodies left in the house, and Placido and Miguelito? Whatever happened to them?"

Anselmo volunteered to finish the story, "When we left the house, we could see the burning fires far away. That night the house burned down. Everyone in San Diego thought the *cabrons* got drunk and passed out until they burned up. Placido and Miguelito never said a word to anyone. There was too much shame, I think. Anyway, both of them have passed. Juan and I are the only ones left."

Tony walked up to them and offered his hand. "Thank you very much for coming," he said. "And thank you for telling us that story. It means a lot to both of us."

Juan was right, Papa Sergio was not a killer. He was a righteous man that had to kill out of necessity. Even though the incident happened before Papa was married and had any children, nobody knew anything about it until that day Anselmo and Juan told Tony and me.

Because of the many opinions that arise out of stories like this, Tony and I decided it would remain a secret. Only to us would the story be known. After all, we knew the nature of men and the disparaging comments that tend to arise from such things. Our families already had the image of Papa Sergio imprinted into their minds, and it was good enough not to molest those images.

It is important to know our Papa Sergio became a mystery to everyone over time—especially after his own death. Nothing made sense as to why he did things until the endgame.

▼ ▼ ▼

Then it came to the time that everyone dreaded. The surviving family had to mass together and sort through all the things Papa Sergio had left behind. There and then we would separate and divide everything into three parts to be equally given to the three remaining daughters.

All the cousins were there for labor purposes, moving things around and doing all of the general leg work. We spent two days separating and dividing among the family; a large part of the estate that was not sold at a garage sale was thrown away. As a collective, if no one claimed it and we couldn't sell it, then we didn't have any choice.

The family put Tony and me in charge of selling or giving away all of the farm and ranch equipment. I wish we could have kept at least some of what we had to sell, but my mother and her two sisters were determined to liquidate everything so they could pay the taxes and put the ranch on the market.

Papa Sergio was right about one thing—his daughters, my mother and her two sisters didn't have enough money to buy the others out in order to save the house and land. Nor did they have the incentive to do so. They may have been raised there on the ranch, but they all traded it for the comforts and conveniences of the big city. I'm sure they couldn't imagine themselves moving back to the old house where they were raised, where horses and goats had to be fed every day.

Even the remaining livestock had to be rounded up and sold. That came to two horses and thirty-five Spanish goats.

We were fortunate because Cade came by with his stock trailer and bought both the horses and all the goats. This made it easier on me and Tony, taking away the burden of having to haul everything to auction and pay a commission to the yard.

Late that afternoon, Cade drove up to the house with his live-stock trailer. It was so hot outside that every time we got close to a water trough, the dogs would jump in the water to cool down. The whole country needed rain. So after Tony and I pushed all of the goats into the pens, we unsaddled the two remaining horses, knowing it was for the last time.

After we loaded all the goats onto his trailer, Cade pulled his rig underneath the shade of a giant oak tree and we took a much-needed break. He pulled out his ice chest full of beer and we all sat down.

"You know? I couldn't get it out of my head what you told me," Cade said, "so I made some phone calls to some of my kinfolks."

"What'd you find out?" Tony asked.

"Only one person knew anything," Cade told us with doubt in his voice.

"Is that it? Only one person?" Tony reaffirmed.

"It's better than no person. The problem is, the information came from my crazy Aunt Joan," Cade said. "In a roundabout way, she told me it was the insurance settlement that paid for the ranch when my grandfather was killed in that plane crash. She said she thought he was hauling a load of untaxed tequila out of Mexico when it happened."

"Tequila? Ah, bullshit!" Tony declared.

"You believe that?" I asked.

"Like I said, Aunt Joan is a little crazy," Cade continued. "The Fergusons ousted her decades ago because she got pregnant at fifteen. Then she ran off with the man that did it—a feed salesman from Colorado. I don't know if any of it is true or not. She's pushing a hundred years old and she was hard to understand."

"That's close enough for me," I told Cade. Then I looked at Tony, "That's got to be his grandfather."

"I agree," said Tony.

"Okay," Cade stood up to rehash the story and think aloud. "So Grandpa Ferguson was the traveling doctor, maybe a dentist, that died in his own plane crash. All the evidence points in the same direction, with the exception that his first name isn't in the newspaper article that printed the crash. You still think that was him?"

"I'd bet money on it," I told Cade.

Tony looked straight at Cade with a serious face, "I would too. And, if that's the case, then Louis and I are the only ones that know more to the story than what the history book says."

"Tony's right. Papa told us the story years ago when we were kids," I revealed, "except the part about smuggling tequila across the border."

"It's a good story," Tony told Cade. "And if it's true, then Papa Sergio probably knew your grandfather."

Cade was frozen in place, trying to soak it all in. Then he downed his beer and announced to us, "Go figure! You'll have to tell me more on another day. I need to get these goats to the ranch before it gets dark. That and Theresa might have my hide."

In no time, Cade was driving out the gate in his screaming Ford diesel. We leaned on the fence and watched him leave.

"Cade's going to shit a brick when we tell him what his grandfather was supposed to be hauling," I told Tony.

"Yeah. And I can't wait to see the look on his face," Tony added.

Tony took the last big gulp of his beer and threw the can into a large barrel. Then he gave me some unexpected news, "When this is over, I'm leaving to see an old army buddy of mine. He lives out west."

"You coming back before you get sent back to Afghanistan?"

"Probably not," Tony revealed. "Don't tell Mom till I'm gone. Okay?"

I looked at him and thought about it. There was nothing I could do or say. I could tell that Tony had already made up his mind.

I reluctantly complied with his request, "Okay, but you're leaving me with a lot of questions to answer from Mom, not to mention the crying that's sure to happen."

Tony took a deep breath, "I know. Just do me that one thing. I'll make everything right later on."

♦ ♦ ♦

By the time Tony and I finished packing all of the tack for sale, the other grandkids had already gone through their assigned buried containers. Now it was time for Tony and me to break the lock on our container. It was late and everyone was gone except Mom. She waited around, thinking we might need her help.

When we finally unlocked the container, it was dark, so we pulled the truck around and pointed the headlights toward the doors of the container, so we could see what we were doing.

Papa Sergio stacked the front half of the container with a multitude of very fancy saddles and horse tack. There were silver-laid western saddles, Mexican saddles, and a collection of valuable spurs and bits that would make any collector envious.

We managed to get everything out with the exception of one item that was sitting on a table in the very back of the container. An old canvas was covering whatever it was.

Tony and I walked up to the table and pulled the canvas off the item with no special expectations. When we did, there it stood before us—a single solid gold statue of an Aztec Eagle Warrior standing three feet tall in all its magnificence of antiquity.

# 18.

## A Venerated Fortune

Inheriting a priceless and venerated object is not simple, nor does it bring only good things. It can be like the lottery winner that watches his life fall apart because he has no discipline. A surge of success can thrust you into a surreal world, testing your faith in men and leaving you with a detrimental dose of paranoia. One must be careful. One must be wise.

♦ ♦ ♦

Needless to say, unveiling the golden Aztec Eagle Warrior was quite a surprise for everyone. It was just as Papa Sergio described it to Tony and me—three feet high and the image of an Aztec warrior in a full eagle headdress with its outstretched eagle wings on one knee, bowing in reverence.

"My God, Luis," Tony said. "It's real."

Sitting on the table next to the Eagle Warrior was the original photograph that Amelia saw, as a reprint, in the Bandera County history book.

Amelia picked it up and looked at it with what little light there was. She confirmed that it was of the *gringo* and the *vaquero* standing next to the small airplane.

"Look at this," she told all of us and passed it around.

Speculation about who was who and why was no longer a consideration. The golden Eagle Warrior and the photo answered a lot of questions.

We saw it as an obvious fact. Dr. Bill Ferguson was both the *gringo* pilot in the picture and Cade's grandfather. Papa Sergio De Zavala was the unknown *vaquero* standing next to Dr. Ferguson. All this time and no one ever recognized him.

It was both of them, Cade's grandfather and my grandfather, who devised the plan to extract one of the fifty golden Aztec Eagle Warriors from an undisclosed cave in Mexico. They created the legend.

My mother ran her fingers over the statue and marveled at its craftsmanship. "All this time, this thing was real. How could I not know?"

"It's not your fault, Mom," Tony tried to comfort her. "Looks like he fooled us all. Who would have known that our own Papa would keep a million-dollar secret for over fifty years?"

I took a good look at the picture and then showed it to Tony, "This picture explains a lot. The Fergusons and the De Zavalas have been associated with each other for a long time."

Tony agreed, "Yeah. There was no first time to meet. Looks like we've known each other for decades." Tony looked at Mom and asked, "Mom? You remember the Fergusons when you were growing up?"

"Sure I do," Mom tried to explain, "but I was born after the Doctor died, I guess. I can't recall any details. I'm ashamed to say it, but I never paid much attention over the years. I was a kid in a world of adults...always being told what to do."

Tony looked at me and asked, "I don't know about you, but I wouldn't feel right about leaving this thing here overnight. Everything else can be locked back up until morning, but the Aztec Warrior needs to go in a giant safe as soon as Monday comes around."

Tony was right and clear in his thinking. We locked everything back up and took the statue to my house.

We placed the golden Eagle Warrior on the kitchen table and made sure all of the windows were covered. Everyone knew that we had to come up with a good plan. But first we needed to take a break. Everyone was excited, yes, but we were exhausted too.

So we covered up the Eagle Warrior with a blanket, ate a decent meal, and went to sleep. Everyone stayed the night at my house.

❧ ❧ ❧

The next day we were all standing in the kitchen and looking at the Eagle Warrior. It had come time for us to decide the fate of this giant hunk of gold.

To bring everybody up to speed, Amelia refreshed our memories of the true gravity of the Eagle Warrior by unraveling the mystery and putting the events into the logical order we could understand. This kind of presentation was right up her alley.

She slowly walked around the statue while holding on to the Bandera County history book.

"So, Dr. Ferguson and Papa Sergio devised a plan for the Doc to fly to Mexico and get the statue while Papa waited for him at his ranch. They were going to split the value of the statue, obviously—except the Doc crashed the plane and died. Papa witnessed the crash but managed to get the Aztec Warrior from the wreckage and didn't tell a soul about it. Then Doc's family made enough money on the insurance policies and bought the now Ferguson Ranch. Meanwhile, Papa disappeared from the scene and never spoke a word to anyone about the find. Later, as his kids had grandchildren, he bought three containers—each one he willed to each set of grandchildren." She paused and looked to us for approval. "That sound right to everyone?"

Everybody agreed with her summary.

Amelia closed her book, sat it down on the table, and casually crossed her arms, "Do you have any idea how hard it must have been to keep a secret like that for...I guess over seventy years? Your Papa Sergio?"

Amelia's comment was well taken. That was one hell of a secret to have kept for such a long period of time. Any other man would have given in to temptation and cashed in on the treasure.

What Tony and I knew about Papa Sergio was something our

other cousins didn't have a clue about. The fact was that Papa was humble and content with what he had. He never appeared to need money. Since the very first day he acquired the golden statue and until the span of the next seventy years, he never cashed it in for its worth. God gave him everything he ever needed. He was never driven by the sin of want or greed.

The same could be said about Tony and I. Ever since we were young, we were never motivated by money. Sure we needed it to survive and navigate the world, but when other things were considered, money and riches were usually number two on the list of importance.

Earlier that day I had called Cade and Theresa. I also called my boss - the wisest man I knew on this matter, Professor Andrew Wilson.

I made it a point, to absolutely not tell either one of them why I needed them to come to the house, just that it was urgent.

That afternoon, Cade and Theresa were the first ones to arrive at the house. After Tony and I made them swear to secrecy under a non-binding and piss-poor structure of an oath, we brought them into the house and watched their eyes widen and mouths drop.

"What in the living hell?" Cade spouted. "Looks like it should be on top of the Arc of the Covenant."

"That looks Aztec," Theresa said and then looked at me, "isn't it?"

I nodded my head, "Yes, it is. And you're not going to believe the story behind it. It starts with your grandfather the dentist, Dr. James Ferguson."

"My grandfather?" Cade said. "Oh, I can't wait to hear this shit!"

"I told you," Tony said aloud.

We all sat down in the living room. Tony and I gave them the whole story while Amelia made sure we didn't make any mistakes. It normally takes a stick of dynamite in Cade's shorts to impress him. The same can also be said about Theresa, but I could tell by the looks on their faces, they were stunned.

Theresa sat there next to Cade the whole time and didn't say a word at first. Finally, she couldn't stand it any longer and she started grinning from ear to ear. Then she covered her mouth and embarrassingly chuckled out of control.

Theresa said under her laugh, "I apologize."

Cade was in a catatonic stare, still looking at me and Tony.

"Any questions?" I cautiously asked him.

"Yeah." Cade looked around the room and then replied, slowly, "Y'all got anything to drink around here? Something that's got a worm in it, maybe?"

Amelia pulled out the airplane photo of Cade's grandfather and Papa Sergio standing next to the plane.

Cade looked it over, "Yep. I guess that *is* them. That was a long time ago. Course, the big question is what you're going to do with that thing in there?"

Before we could answer there was a sudden knock at the door that startled everyone. It was Andrew Wilson, just the man I needed to see.

Wilson walked through the front door wearing his work clothes, which included his straw hat. He was still encrusted in the dirt and sweat from the dig I was supposed to be supervising that day. Instead, I called him earlier that morning and told him it was important enough to take the day off if he wanted to but imperative for him to come to my house that very day. When he asked me why, just like Cade and Theresa, I wouldn't tell him over the phone.

Theresa went up to him and offered her hand, "Mr. Andrew Wilson, my name is Theresa Ferguson and this is my husband, Cade. We actually met years ago."

"We have?" Wilson reacted with surprise.

"During the Bowie knife incident at the capital," she revealed.

Wilson's eyes lit up, "Oh yeah! That day could have ruined me. Lucky for me, I had some good people on my side." Wilson looked at me, "Well? I came as soon as I could. I could tell by the way you were talking it must be important."

"You're going to be shocked," Tony said.

"Don't worry, Mr. Wilson," Cade announced, "Theresa and I both know CPR."

Wilson's attention as he lost his grin and stared at Cade for a moment. Then we moved to the kitchen.

Everyone agreed not to tell a soul about the golden Eagle Warrior until we talked to Andrew Wilson. When it came to archeology, he was by far the wisest man I knew. He had a working knowledge of what a cultural artifact of this significance could have upon the custodians.

Then there was the other thing I tried not to talk about because I found it hard to explain to other people. I considered the golden Aztec Eagle Warrior a spiritual and volatile artifact. You can bet your ass that son-of-a-bitch was haunted before Tony and I unveiled it, and it was still haunted while it sat there on my kitchen table. I didn't want it in my house. Perhaps the burden it caused me would have been less if it was made of stone, but it wasn't. It was made of solid gold and worth a small fortune.

The responsibility of being its caretaker was not something I enjoyed. I wanted to get rid of it as soon as I got the damn thing. It gave me the same kind of anxiety I had when I acquired the Black Heart Stone.

Tony and I discussed this and both of us agreed. We needed to rid ourselves of it responsibly and make sure it came to rest in a proper place.

Wilson stared at the statue and sighed, "If I hadn't seen it with my own two eyes, I wouldn't have believed it. Aztec?"

"Yep," I confirmed.

"And surrounded by lost souls and imps," Wilson mumbled.

"There are supposed to be forty-nine identical statues where this one came from," I added.

Wilson looked at me with a surprised look on his face, "Forty-nine? Ho-ly crap! Have you weighed this thing?"

"It's a hair over seventy-two pounds," Tony said.

Wilson pulled out his calculator and started punching numbers, "The gold alone is worth over a million and a half, but a museum would gladly pay you double—maybe triple."

Everyone gasped at the amount.

Wilson squinted up his face and looked me straight in the eyes. With a serious face, he asked me, "Please tell me that this is not work-related, Luis."

"It's not," I assured him. "Believe it or not, we inherited it from our grandfather. Let's go and sit down in the living room, Andrew. It's a long story."

Theresa stopped him before he got too far, "Mr. Wilson, what did you mean, lost souls and imps?"

Wilson tried explaining it without alarming the senses, but it still came out sounding like a prophetic warning of impending doom. "This thing came from an Aztec sacrificial chamber. Thousands died in its presence. Lost souls will protect the only thing they remember from the world they remember. They are wayward ghosts and demons to you and me, Mrs. Ferguson. Believe me, if something bad hasn't happened yet, it will. The sooner you get rid of that thing, the better."

"So what are we supposed to do until we do get rid of it?" asked Amelia.

"Stay humble. Stay reverent," Wilson concluded.

I spent the next thirty minutes telling Wilson the story about the Aztec Warrior statue. Tony and Amelia made sure I didn't leave anything out. When I told him we needed his advice, he didn't waste any time.

He looked at Mom and asked, "Mrs. Anna, are you going to make any kind of legal claim for ownership of the statue?"

"No," Mom told him.

Then Wilson looked at Cade and Theresa, "How about you, Cade? Are you or Theresa going to make a claim to ownership or profits?"

"Not a chance," Cade said.

"They're family, Mr. Wilson," Theresa told him with proud confidence. "We wouldn't do that."

"That's good to hear," continued Wilson, "but not all families see this sort of thing the way you do."

Mom looked at me and Tony, "He's right, *mijos*. I love my sisters and all, but this could change things."

Wilson stood up from his chair, put his hand in his pockets, and lowered his head. Then he began to slowly walk in circles in the middle of the living room floor. He was deep in calculations.

"The first thing to do is get a certificate of ownership. It's easy to do, and you can file it down at the courthouse all in the same day. All you need is a few signatures. Secondly, get the Eagle Warrior to the bank so they can put it in their vault. Then I'd feel safe about telling your family what was in your container. And Luis, Tony, get ready to stand your ground. One of them might make a claim...maybe even take you to court."

"That's a disheartening thought," Amelia commented.

"What if we didn't tell them anything at all?" Tony asked.

"No one looks the same the day after they become millionaires, Tony," Wilson told him. "Sure as hell, they'll find out one way or another and you'll have more problems. It's the moral thing to do." Then he looked at me, "Have you got plans? You know what you want to do with it?"

I glanced at Tony and then back at Wilson, "We've already talked about it. We decided we want to sell it to a museum."

"Luis and I are going to take the money," Tony looked at Mom, "and buy the family ranch before we lose it."

Mom's face immediately turned emotional, but she put her hands over her mouth and tried not to interrupt things by crying.

"Well. You'll have enough. That's for sure," Wilson assured us.

"How do we go about getting this thing sold?" Tony asked.

"Luis knows. We've both done this before with the Black Heart Stone, but first things first," Wilson continued, "let me take some pictures and document its existence, then get this thing to a bank vault somewhere and use an armored truck to do it. Don't take any chances on something going wrong while it's in your hands. Secure the Aztec Warrior, and then I'll help you find a buyer. That'll be no problem."

"We can do that," Tony said.

"I just got one question," Wilson asked, "maybe two."

"What's that?" I asked.

"Since you're going to be a rich man after this, are you going to quit your job," Wilson asked cautiously, "and make me look for a replacement?"

"No," I answered, "I'd like to stay if you will still have me."

"Yes. I would," Wilson said and then turned his attention towards Tony. "What about you, Tony? You going to stay?"

"I don't think so, Mr. Wilson," Tony said. "I got family here, yeah. But I got a kind of brotherhood in the army too. I can't walk away. Not now."

Andrew Wilson looked at Mom for a moment and smiled, "You got some good sons, Anna."

Needless to say, Mom was very happy when she heard Tony say that we were going to buy the ranch. For the past twenty years she had been mentally preparing herself to lose the very home she grew up on.

♥ ♥ ♥

After Wilson left the house, Amelia poked me in the ribs. She was trying to get my attention. When I inadvertently ignored her and started to talk to Cade, she got right in front of me and grimaced, "This is a good time. Tell your mother." She ordered me.

"Tell me what?" Mom asked.

"Tell her," Amelia demanded of me again.

So I looked at Mom with a straight face and said, "Mom, when we get this thing sold, we're going to pay off your house in town."

"You won't have to work if you don't want to," Tony proudly told her.

It was a sight I'll never forget as long as I live. Mom's face was grinning from ear to ear. She came up to me and Tony and gave us the kind of big tight hugs that only a mother knows how to do. And then she started crying, "Thank you," she told both of us, over and over again, "Thank you!"

I guess I'm not a very sensitive man because while all the girls were tearing up and having an emotional breakthrough, all I could think about was a bucket of fried chicken and cold beer.

It was too late in the day to get an armored truck out to the house, so I made arrangements for a security company to come out the next morning.

Everything we did that day took the entire day. We had stayed together long enough to tell the story of the Aztec Warrior twice and make tentative plans for its future.

I got everyone's attention and spoke up, "Okay! I don't know about y'all but I'm tired of being so serious for so long. I say we go get some food and drinks and celebrate right here at the house—in the shadow of the golden Aztec Eagle Warrior."

Make no doubt about eating and drinking together when it came to family or friends, those times of celebration were the best moments in our lives. It always strengthened the bonds between family and friends.

🔻 🔻 🔻

The next day an armored truck showed up at the house and they loaded the golden Aztec Eagle Warrior. As soon as they closed and locked the doors, the air conditioner went out on their armored truck.

Since they had the Aztec warrior loaded, they were committed by the contract and couldn't take it back out. So they drove forty-five miles to the bank with the windows rolled up, and it was hot as hell.

We followed them to the bank, and by the time the security guards opened the doors, they were soaked in sweat. It was a miracle they didn't all have a heat stroke.

Was it an imp that caused this? Maybe.

The guards rolled the Aztec Warrior into the bank on a dolly that was made to move refrigerators and washing machines. Although the statue was covered so no one could see what it was, the instant the statue rolled onto the floor of the vault, the entire bank lost electricity. For no reason the power in the entire city block went out, making the emergency battery backup system cut on.

When the front doors automatically locked themselves and the bank alarm went off, half of the bank employees started freaking out. The knee-jerk reaction was that there was a robbery in progress. After the manager quickly turned off the alarm and assured them everything was okay, he had to do the same thing with the police at the front door a few minutes later.

That wouldn't have been such a big deal except when the front doors locked, the security guards went into an instant panic. Not because of the alarm itself, but because they had left the back doors of the armored car wide open when the front doors to the bank automatically locked. And the armored truck was still running with the keys in it.

It was a good thing honest people were in town that day because there were thousands in coinage in unguarded plain sight for the taking. Luckily for them, the manager came to their rescue when he unlocked the doors.

Was this the works of the wayward spirits that caused everything to go wrong? My money was on the spirits.

🔻 🔻 🔻

The next day Tony and I went back to the bank and showed the manager our certificate of ownership for the statue. He was a short dumpy guy with a bald head. The kind of a person that saved a portion of his lunch money every day for his entire life until he had enough to buy a used car with mice in the glove compartment. An ace at math and anything that had numbers in it, no wonder he got the be the manager of a bank. In his profession, not much excitement ever happened. Then we showed him the Eagle Warrior behind the closed doors of the safety deposit vault.

"Drop my drawers and call me shorty!" the banker said. "Is it solid gold?"

"Yep," Tony acknowledged.

"What are you going to do with it?" the banker asked. "Leave it here? Cash it in?"

"We're going to sell it to a museum," I told him.

The banker looked rather excited at that point, so he asked, "Are y'all going to bank here at this bank?"

Tony and I looked at each other and nodded in agreement.

"Sure," I told him.

Then the banker got down on his knees and took a closer look. He was marveling at it, "I tell you what, you keep it here until it sells. Bank here like you said and I'll give you a million-dollar line of credit as of today."

What a deal! We went for the offer hook, line, and sinker.

Tony and I took the line of credit and summoned the other part of the De Zavalas for the big meeting. I chose the biggest restaurant I could find for the family to have the meeting. Knowing what I was going to tell them, there was a small chance that something could go sideways. They would be less tempted if we were all in the public eye when Tony and I announced it.

The one thing that was in our favor was the fact that Papa Sergio's will had already been probated in court. It was final and binding. Every item in each container was already in the possession of the inheritors. Our small worry was that someone would make an unfounded proclamation for ownership and we would have a new set of troubles.

I told the story to everyone of how we opened up the container and unveiled the golden Aztec Eagle Warrior. When I finished, no one said a word. All of my extended family just stared at me.

The blunt fact was that none of the other containers had anything remotely similar to what Tony and I inherited. We got the most, and it was the biggest.

Our two aunts were satisfied with the story and didn't complain, but for just a second I thought our cousins would. Some of them insisted on knowing what we were going to spend so much money on. I could sense a little jealousy in the air.

Then Ignacio broke the tension by asking, "Hey *Primo!* You think I could borrow some money to buy a freezer? I got all this dried mule meat and don't know where to put it."

We knew then that everything was good between us and the cousins. It was a good feeling to have. I was afraid that our instant wealth might cause a rift in the De Zavala family.

Then Tony stood up from the table and got everyone's attention. He told them of our plans, "Luis and I are going to buy and co-own Papa's ranch. That way, it will stay in the family for all of the De Zavalas to use. Just as it's always been."

Aunt Evangelina and Aunt Monica began to cry over their empty dinner plates. All their adult lives they had been resigned, just like our mother, to the fact that someday they would be forced to relinquish their childhood home because of forces beyond their control. Things changed for them in an instant. Tony, Amelia, and I hit a home run that day.

Tony refused to make a claim on the big house. Since Amelia was pregnant, he thought we'd need all the room we could get. And someday, he would be back. Maybe to build his own house on the ranch or not. There was no rush.

🔻 🔻 🔻

Andrew Wilson managed to find a buyer for the golden Aztec Eagle Warrior. It was a big museum that had a lot of money. After the transaction was completed, the whereabouts of the statue sort of disappeared for a while. I guess the museum had to straighten out some details. Like how to fight the mischievous demons that hovered about causing chaos where ever it was taken.

After things slowed down a little, I tried to take everything in and come back to reality. I wanted to become a normal man on the street again because of my wife Amelia and my unborn child.

Looking back, I seriously doubt that Tony or I could have handled everything so wisely if we had inherited such a cache of riches when we were younger. I could see from anywhere I stood that failure was but a breath away from us the whole time. But we stayed true to one another and never gave in to the lure of shiny things.

Papa Sergio was preparing us all those years, and we didn't have a clue why or what he was doing. Preparing us not to simply inherit the Golden Warrior but to uphold the integrity of the family name. Papa made us promise not to be swayed by the iniquities of men and to stay on the true straight path. Tony and I did our best to stay true to our upbringings.

But lo and behold the realities of the real world can bring storms without warnings and test the goodness of men.

# 19.

## Back to the Front

We all realized something about the same time. As soon as the final piece of furniture went into the big house on Wednesday, the next day we would be the legal owners of the ranch. However, nobody wanted to celebrate that night. Everyone was totally exhausted and we all turned in early. It was our first night in our permanent home and I have never felt more contented.

When we awoke the next morning, the title of new ownership of the De Zavala Ranch was officially passed down from Papa Sergio to us, his grandsons, Luis and Antonio. With the tools and blessings we were afforded, we succeeded by keeping the ranch in the family.

❦　❦　❦

Early morning was to become my morning ritual—a cup of coffee and a few steps out of the door, I would systematically stroll across the porch and lean on one of the support beams. From there I could see and marvel at the life gathering around the water troughs and pens. All life thirsts for drink. All life was hungry.

The sun had just broken the horizon. The air was still cool from lingering winter, and there were so many sounds of birds singing in the air and smells that only a ranch can produce.

As I discovered, there was wildlife all around me every day. Water being a constant source of attraction for all animals, it seemed that all preferred our water in the trough over the creek water nearby.

The spilled feed that's poured in the troughs for the horses and goats was an opportunistic source of extra nutrition for all the smaller animals that needed a little more. If the birds didn't find the spilled grain, sometimes it had a chance to sprout into sprigs.

Then there's the squirrels and the wild hogs and the raccoons and the opossums and even the snakes—and you know, I loved it. The ranch gave me purpose and made me feel more alive.

The good thing about the big house was the front porch. It went around three-quarters of the house and had an old-fashioned dog run right smack dab in the middle. There was a porch swing, a small table, and several fly swatters within reach of every chair.

While I was standing on the porch and marveling at the landscape, Tony came out the door carrying his duffel bag.

"Not going to West Texas?" I asked, but really, I knew.

"Nope," Tony said. "Becoming a millionaire took too much time. Next time, maybe."

This time, something was different. I could tell that Tony was trying to avoid eye contact with me.

"You say bye to Amelia?" I asked, but knew the answer to that too.

"Yea," then he looked off into the distance in thought. "She started crying. I guess it's those hormones from being pregnant."

I nodded my head, "I think she loves her brother-in-law...like her husband."

Tony looked at me and tried to smile, but I could see it was difficult. He only looked me in the eye for a brief second, spending those last moments gazing upon the ground for some reason. I didn't know why, but I wasn't going to push him where he didn't want to go either. He was having a hard enough time fighting back the tears.

So I tried to ease things a bit, "I'll let you know when she foals," referring to when Amelia gives birth.

We both laughed again and he gave me a brother's hug. Then he simply turned around and walked down the steps until he reached his old pickup truck.

As he threw his duffel bag in the bed of the truck, I gave him the only advice I knew of about Afghanistan, "Watch out for those giant man-eating spiders you told us about. You better check your luggage before you come back home. Don't want none of those pinche sons-of-bitches around here. We got enough problems with Daddy Long Legs."

Tony leaned on the truck bed, still looking into his truck bed, and tried to laugh unsuccessfully. Then just as quickly, his smile vanished again. Slowly he turned towards me and walked up to the bottom of the porch and looked me dead in the eyes. At that moment, the air became stale. Everything changed in an instant, and then I heard every word of the story he told me. It was a jolt.

"I killed two of our own guys, Luis," Tony confessed. "I wasn't always *that* engineer, you know. Sometimes they sent us out on foot patrols when they were short on foot patrols. Most of the time nothing ever happened, but one day we caught some of our own torturing an Iraqi civilian."

I tried to reserve my volume. I couldn't help myself, "Holy smokes, Tony?"

Tony started shaking his head, "Honestly, we didn't know whether or not this guy was a terrorist Taliban or not—hell, he probably deserved to die as far I knew. Anyway, my squad leader challenged them on the matter and he was shouted down. What did we know? We were engineers. After an exchange of "fuck yous," one of them pulled his pistol and shot that poor bastard right in the head."

"Sweet Jesus!" I said.

Tony was trembling as he told the story. I could see that he didn't like to recall what happened. Now I could see why he was keeping this a secret for so long and never told a soul. As his brother, I wasn't about to abandon him. I was going to ride that bucking horse with him to the bitter end.

"Things got out of hand," Tony continued. "One of theirs shot into our squad—so I shot back. One of ours was wounded. I killed two of theirs. Our own guys."

Tony took a few good deep breaths and then things seemed to

get better, but not until a few silent moments passed to regain himself.

"Is it over?" I asked, "I mean...you know."

"For right now. There was an investigation, but there might be a court martial later. I don't know," Tony said.

"Those guys in West Texas, the friends of yours, they were there?" I asked.

"Yeah."

"Sounds like you did the right thing. Surely the army can see that?" I asked, trying to find some relief in the situation.

"You would think so," Tony stated in theory.

I tried to assure him in the only way I could think of, "Otherwise, you'd be in a cell somewhere. That's what I'd figure anyway."

Tony agreed and nodded, "Yeah, well, the army ain't exactly known for being logical."

"I know you probably don't want to hear it, but now you got enough money, I would think, to buy a good lawyer and get out of the army," I added.

I pushed Tony's honor button and he was not fine with it. It challenged his integrity as I knew it would. Furthermore, he knew I knew better than to ask that question.

My brother gave me a stern look and made sure I understood, "I'm not going to run away, and you know it, Luis. If I'm not there to stand up and be counted with the rest of them," he shook his head and looked into the bed of his pickup truck, "somebody will brand me as a murderer."

"Yeah. I guess so."

"I'm not a killer, Luis," he said. "I'm just a man in a camouflaged uniform that wants to be a geologist. Now more than ever."

There wasn't much to say after that.

"I'll take care of your horse while you're gone," I told him as a final assurance.

I watched Tony drive his truck away and rumble over the cattle-guard, kicking up dust the whole way until he reached the main road. Oddly enough, I never had the reaction to move from where I was standing. Even after his truck was out of sight and the dust had already settled, I remained in that one spot and thought about what he told me.

Familiar thoughts were going through my head again. Questions about the sum total of our efforts that got us where we were.

Not many families had the relationship that my brother and I had with one another. It's a closeness and understanding that could never be measured on any scale. Once I had thought of his thinking process as the same as a squirrel, but I never thought that of him again. There are few like him. The same can be said for Amelia, who became my De Zavala wife and an unexpected gem of the family.

Tony would come back from the war one day a full but more serious and resolute man. He would take that trip to see his army buddies in West Texas.

Never electing for the comforts of this world, he made it a habit to plunge into the jaws of adversity, living one adventure after another.

Hard times would be in store for all of us in the future. We would all survive but not without first undergoing the trials and tribulations of our journeys. It's inevitable, and yet sometimes painful, the steps that everyone must deal with, or roll over and expose your belly to the sky in submission.

If I am ever tested to such ends again, without question things will be different. Because this time I can vouch for my soul, for I know who I am. My name is Luis Manuel and I am the descendant of great men that were great teachers. I am of the house of De Zavala.

# The End

*Lorenzo De Zavala. Engraving portrait with signature.*
*Registro Yucateco, Toma 3, 1846*

# Lorenzo De Zavala

Lorenzo De Zavala y Sanchez was born October 3, 1788 and died November 15, 1836. Better known to history as simply Lorenzo De Zavala, he was born in Tecoh, Yucatán when Mexico was under Spanish rule, and educated in Mérida, the Yucatecan capital. After graduating from the *Tridentine Seminary of San Ildefonso* he founded his own newspaper, *El Aristarco Universal* (The Universal Critic). Highly critical of the Spanish government, De Zavala was sentenced to three years in prison for his writing. While in jail, he learned the English language and studied medical textbooks. Upon his release, he became a physician, politician and diplomat, as well as an author. De Zavala was highly intellectual and fluent in several languages.

After Mexico gained its independence from Spain in 1824, De Zavala helped draft the constitution for the First Federal Republic of Mexico. In 1836, he contributed to the drafting of the constitution for the newly independent Republic of Texas—Mexico's enemy at the time. He later became the first vice president of the Republic of Texas under Sam Houston.

A county and a city are named in De Zavala's honor, as well as many schools and public buildings, including the Texas State Archives and Library Building in Austin.

Lorenzo De Zavala was a rock star in his time. It's just too bad that a year after the Republic of Texas declared its independence, Lorenzo fell out of a boat in Buffalo Bayou, caught pneumonia, and died so soon in life. Fortunately, what he left was a legacy of accomplishments along with his good name.

It is a chapter in history that we should never forget, and yet if you ask people on the street, most do not know Lorenzo De Zavala. Maybe with a little more emphasis on history for our children, we could all change that.

All the wealth and comforts we have here in Texas are the result of *Tejanos* that pushed for change far before the northern settlers like Stephen Austin migrated to the state. Tejanos, on the other hand, were born and lived under the dictatorships of Spain and then Santa Anna. At that time, no one had illusions about what tyrannical governments were capable of.

# The Author

When he was ten years old, Mike Lowrie and his younger brother ran away from home, not with the intent to join the circus, but for the adventure. That's how it all started.

Born and raised in Texas, he grew up in the region of East Texas that included cotton fields and the famed piney woods of the Nacogdoches area. He spent his boyhood in a rural life, hunting, fishing and exploring. In 1972, he moved to San Antonio, where he graduated from John Marshall High School and then joined the U.S. Army. He spent a total of four years as a military policeman, then later, ten years in the U.S. Coast Guard Reserve.

He attended Sam Houston State University in Huntsville and the University of Texas in San Antonio. In 1985, Mike joined Buffalo Bill's Wild West Show as a trick roper and horse trainer. In 1986, he was hired as an assistant wagon master for the Texas Wagon Train Sesquicentennial Celebration.

As a civilian he worked as a cowboy, oilfield roughneck, truckdriver, lawman and owned and ran his own construction business for over twenty years.

Now retired and living in Bandera County, Mike Lowrie writes books, incorporating his experiences into stories that take place mostly in Texas.

Printed in the USA
CPSIA information can be obtained
at www.ICGtesting.com
JSHW082047140923
48476JS00001BA/4